NEW WAW

SAHARAN OASIS

MODERN MIDDLE EAST
LITERATURES IN TRANSLATION SERIES

NEW WAW

SAHARAN OASIS

IBRAHIM AL-KONI

TRANSLATED AND INTRODUCED
BY WILLIAM M. HUTCHINS

CENTER FOR MIDDLE EASTERN STUDIES
THE UNIVERSITY OF TEXAS AT AUSTIN

Cover Art: Cover image provided courtesy of the artist, Hawad.
Copyediting, Cover and Text Design: Kristi Shuey
Series Editor: Wendy E. Moore

Library of Congress Control Number: 2013950932
ISBN: 978-0-292-75475-1

This translation was made from the second Arabic edition of *Waw al-Sughra*
(Beirut: al-Mu'assasa al-'Arabiya li-l-Dirasat wa-l-Nashr, 1999).

The first two chapters of this translation appeared in *Banipal* 40 (Spring 2011).

The National Endowment for the Arts awarded a literary translation grant for 2012
to support the translation of this novel.

TABLE *of* CONTENTS

CHARACTERS

Ababa: a member of the Council of Nobles

Aggulli: a sage and leader

Ahallum the Hero: the tribe's warrior

Amasis the Younger: a noble elder

Asaruf: a noble elder

Diviner or Soothsayer: the leader's confidant

Ejabbaran: noble elder, sage

Emmamma: a noble elder, eventually the oldest man
in the tribe and its venerable elder

Enigmatic Stranger: Wantahet or one of his avatars

Excavator: a stranger who travels with the tribe and
digs his "tent" in the belly of the earth

Imaswan Wandarran: spokesman for the Council of Nobles

Leader: a poet in love with a female poet but condemned
to lead a Tuareg tribe

Lover of Stones: the tribe's master builder

Virgin, Tomb Maiden, Temple Maiden, Priestess:
the Leader's posthumous bride and his medium

Wantahet: a figure from Tuareg folklore

INTRODUCTION

In an interview with Scott Simon on National Public Radio, the Appalachian author Ron Rash said: "Landscape is very often destiny" for a writer and referred to "literature of landscape."[1] The landscape of the Sahara Desert has certainly been destiny for Ibrahim al-Koni, and his novel *New Waw: Saharan Oasis* contrasts the landscapes and cultures of desert nomadism with those of oasis life.

Al-Koni has written that, from the time of his descent from the high desert plateaus to start his formal schooling at twelve, he has felt a mission to speak for the desert, to help it make "its own statement, which had not yet been enunciated." Melville had spoken for the sea, Dostoyevsky for the city, and Antoine de Saint-Exupéry had even spoken for space. "Only the desert has not yet offered its statement." So, when he began to write in the mid 1960s, what was essential was to express the desert. At the same time, though, he points out that "Every reader of my works quickly perceives that the desert I am talking about is a metaphor for the world, an allegory for the world."[2]

Ibrahim al-Koni, a Tuareg whose mother tongue is Tamasheq, is an international author with many identities. He is an award-winning Arabic-language novelist who has already published more than seventy volumes, a Moscow-educated visionary who sees an inevitable interface between myth and contemporary life, an environmentalist, and a Saharan writer who depicts desert life with great accuracy and emotional depth while layering it with mythical and literary references the way a painter might apply luminous washes to a canvas.

His elegant, formal Arabic can be complex and suggests a clear and simple but still formal English rendition, with an occasional modern word added to rouse the reader from any mythical slumber. The description in *New Waw* of the excavator's love affair with the earth in the original Arabic is a virtuoso piece of lyrical Arabic prose.

---

1. Ron Rash, "'Nothing Gold' Stays Long In Appalachia," *Weekend Edition*, National Public Radio, February 16, 2013.
2. Ibrahim al-Koni, "Le 'discours' du desert: Témoinage," in *La poétique de l'espace dans la littérature arabe moderne*, ed. Boutros Hallaq, Robin Ostle, and Stefan Wild (Paris: Presses Sorbonne Nouvelle, 2002), 96–101.

Chapter XII contains a memorable landscape painted with words. In a chapter devoted to al-Koni's work, Ziad Elmarsafy has described his language as "highly stylized Arabic."[3]

Ibrahim al-Koni's political fiction is philosophical, and readers occasionally remark that some of his novels, like *New Waw*, are intellectually challenging at several levels of meaning. There are a number of words that al-Koni has used systematically in multiple novels till they have become technical terms. These include words like *al-khafa'* or Spirit World, *al-khala'* or the wasteland, *al-'arraf* (feminine: *al-'arrafa*) for diviner, and *al-tih* for the desert's labyrinth.

Al-Koni does not simply take his readers on an adventurous trip through the Sahara but embeds them in a culture in which the natural world is rife with signs, symbols, sparks of enlightenment, and prophecies. A senile bird is a sign. When the migratory birds leave the nomads' encampment, diviners follow the flocks to search for the prophecy encoded in their trajectories. The master mason explains to the diviner in *New Waw* that "We have a duty to discover the symbol in everything."

The Tuareg, or Kel Tamasheq, are a traditionally pastoralist, nomadic Berber people, who have moved freely across the Sahara from Libya, Tunisia, Algeria to Mauritania, Mali, Niger, and Burkina Faso. Today national boundaries and policies hinder their migrations, and there have been armed Tuareg insurrections in Mali and Niger. In April 2012, an independent state of Azawad was proclaimed in three northern districts of Mali—Kidal, Gao, and Timbuktu—by Tuareg rebels reinforced by arms from Libya. In January 2013 France led an offensive to retake the north of Mali from the Islamists who had pushed aside their Tuareg allies.

The Tuareg language is Tamasheq (also known as Tamahaq), which has its own alphabet, Tifinagh, that dates back at least to the third century BCE. Evidence of Arabic-Tamasheq bilingualism among the Tuareg in Mali goes back hundreds of years in the form of inscriptions and graffiti.[4] Currently there is at least one other Tuareg novelist writing in Arabic: Umar al-Ansari.[5]

---

3. Ziad Elmarsafy, *Sufism in the Contemporary Arabic Novel* (Edinburgh: Edinburgh University Press, 2012), 107.
4. P. F. de Moraes Farias, *Arabic Medieval Inscriptions from the Republic of Mali* (Oxford & New York: Oxford University Press for the British Academy, 2003), cxxvii *ff.*
5. Umar al-Ansari, *Tabib Tinbuktu* [*The Physician of Timbuktu*] (Beirut: al-Mu'assasa al-'Arabiya li-l-Dirasat wa-l-Nashr, 2012).

The Tuareg have been affiliated with Islam for centuries, but the goddess Tanit is invoked several times in *New Waw* and traditional Tuareg life has been governed by a tribal code of law, even though its written text is no longer extant. In his novels al-Koni refers to this lost law as al-Namus, perhaps to distinguish it from the Islamic Shari'ah.

The oasis novels by al-Koni trace the development, flourishing, and destruction of an oasis community named in honor of the Tuareg people's lost oasis, the paradise-like Waw (pronounced approximately like the English word "wow"). This "distant oasis lying beyond every other oasis" still occasionally appears to a few visionaries who are not looking for it. Al-Koni, who welcomes multiple allusions, has also referred to it as another Atlantis.[6]

New Waw (*Waw al-Sughra*, 1997, more literally Little Waw or Lesser Waw) is the first book in a trilogy that continues with *The Puppet* (*al-Dumya*, 1998) and *The Scarecrow* (*al-Fazza'a*, 1998). A putative fourth volume is *The Tumor* (*al-Waram*, 2008), although these books have been published and marketed separately in Arabic.

New Waw describes the birth and growth of this oasis in the Sahara, and major characters like the venerable elder Emmamma, the warrior Ahallum, and the sage Aggulli (also Aghulli) are introduced here. *The Puppet* chronicles the community's peak of prosperity and therefore also the beginning of its decline. The eponymous character of *The Scarecrow* may appear in one or more guises in *New Waw* and is an enigmatic, apparently benign character in *The Puppet*. Finally in *The Scarecrow* this avatar of the Tuareg mythic figure Wantahet supervises the destruction of New Waw, reveling in his self-righteous sadism. When the oasis is under siege from international forces, he masterminds the killing of its inhabitants and then morphs back into the scarecrow.

From a nomadic point of view, any settlement—even for pressing reasons of leadership succession and even in a model oasis community like New Waw—is subversive and a disruption of the traditional nomadic ethos, according to which endless migration provides a geographical cure.[7]

In West Africa, Islamic societies have retained elements of pre-Islamic cultures for extended periods, and Sufism has been an important strand

6. Al-Koni, "Témoinage," 98.
7. See Michael Parker, *The Geographical Cure* (New York: Penguin Books, 1994) for an American exploration of the curative virtues of travel or migration.

in the Islamic tapestry there. Tuareg spirituality as depicted in al-Koni's fiction is also multifaceted. The inhabitants of the Spirit World, many of whom are jinn (genies), maintain an uneasy truce with their Tuareg neighbors. (As in other parts of Islamic West Africa, in Tuareg lands the jinn recall earlier folk gods.) Like the author, al-Koni's heroes typically feel a special bond with their ancient ancestors and the Saharan rock inscriptions they left behind. In novels like *Anubis* and *The Seven Veils of Seth*, al-Koni added ancient Egyptian ingredients to his spiritual stew. The deceased leader's rule over the tribe and *New Waw*'s two-chapter sequence in which the tribe's diviner travels in the Western Hammada with the deceased leader parallel the role in many traditional African folk religions of the Living Dead, who are ancestors in the Spirit World. They keep close tabs on their living descendants, advising them in dreams and visions, through a medium, or by visiting in person if necessary. The preoccupation in the middle of the novel with spirit possession and sorcery and antidotes to them are other parallels to traditional African folk religious practices.[8]

Tensions between nomadism and settled life in al-Koni's novels have implications beyond Tuareg (or Mongolian) nomadism; they affect all of us when we face choices like relocation for career advancement. If scientists model human medical conditions on laboratory animals and breed special families of creatures for their research, and if other researchers use one phenomenon as a model for another, al-Koni may be said to create models derived from Saharan life for the study of assorted global issues. If al-Koni has frequently used similar Saharan models, he has deployed them at least in part as metaphors for a wide spectrum of human concerns. All the same, his models are lovingly based on Tuareg folklore, about which he is a leading expert. Although many of his novels seem allegorical, they are better described as reverse allegories: excellent examples of many different things offered for the reader's creative use. One reader may, for example, choose to consider the almost Satanic leader in *The Tumor* and *The Scarecrow* as an allusion to Colonel Qaddafi, and the brave new community of New Waw may stand for Libya. Another equally perceptive reader may be brooding about some other time or place.

---

8. See Benjamin C. Ray, *African Religions: Symbol, Ritual, and Community,* 2nd ed. (Upper Saddle River, New Jersey: Prentice Hall, 2000) for information about these.

If the message of *New Waw* were distilled into one phrase it might be that enhanced insight into the human condition is not neatly correlated with technological progress. Fortunately *New Waw* is a novel and not a distilled message.

William M. Hutchins

NEW WAW
SAHARAN OASIS

I

THE WINGED PEOPLE

What? Didn't you say the sky and birds prove God's existence?

Blaise Pascal, *Pensées*, Article IV, Section 244

1

For as long as he could remember he had listened for counterpoint in the bird's song.

In fact, after many seasons had elapsed and the gullies had experienced numerous floods, he felt certain now that this hidden bird's polyphonic skill was the secret reason he had been fascinated with it over the years. The bird's soft, gentle call, which reminded him of wind whistling through reeds, could not be transcribed in any script nor could the tongue mimic it. It began as a faint murmur, and then a mournful cooing immediately came in and rose to a robust melody that sounded like the vibrations of the *imzad*'s lone,[1] mournful string harmonizing with a second, lower string. These two then blended together to create—sadly, mournfully, and lyrically—an epic that told the entire desert's story. The secretive call created an equally secret message. The song, which could not be recorded by an alphabet or even pictographs and which thwarted any attempt by a tongue to imitate it, began with a soft, mild, mysterious, nebulous murmur that stirred longing and that—as it grew ever louder—breathed life into concealed embers, into sparks that have always been the wayfarer's law and that have always served as the religion of the wasteland's inhabitants, who, since their birth, have never stopped searching for what the wasteland has hidden. The bird's call suddenly became polyphonic as another concealed bird joined in, and then this new voice keened a different ballad. The two melodies created a counterpoint and harmonized to become a single tune, a new carol. Then the song changed course and soared into another realm, transforming the bare land and extending its expanse. The wasteland's temptation grew ever more intense, and the desert promised a new reunion, an everlasting one that was born the same day the wayfarer was and that burst into existence the same day he did, even though the wayfarer would depart and wander off while the promise remained. The eternal temptation endured as a hint of an impossible reunion and functioned as a huge snare to lure wayfarers to the desert and to life by flaunting a promise—of an oasis and a reunion—that would never be fulfilled. In the newly expanded distance, delight triumphed and the heart overflowed with ecstasy. The

---

1. A bowed, single-stringed Tuareg instrument traditionally played by women.

body quivered with a dancelike tremor, because a glow had appeared on the horizon, because a torch had cleft the dark recesses of the pale, eternal horizon, appearing for a brief glimpse as a flash of lightning, and this was a sign the wayfarer had craved for a long time and had struggled endlessly to observe. Then the stern, hostile, eternal emptiness supplied a signal like sparks of revelation, and he saw what he had never seen in that expanse and discovered what he had never been able to find; in fact, he discovered what he had not wanted to find.

So how could his frail body keep from trembling ecstatically? How could a tear of longing not spill from his eye?

2

The desert welcomes birds twice a year. In the spring, flocks arrive from the South, spend a few days in the nomadic encampments, and then call to each other to resume their voyage to the countries of the North. In fall, they come from the North, spend some days in the camps again, and then call to each other to travel to the lands of the South. People say that in the past the flocks preferred oases as migratory way stations but that these dense throngs of birds alarmed the oasis dwellers, who thought the onslaught threatened their crops. So they fought off the birds, set traps for them, shot arrows at them, and beat drums to frighten them away. Then the birds abandoned the oases, and migrating flocks avoided cultivated fields, eventually choosing the desert's nomadic camps for their stopovers. The desert people consider their arrival a very good omen, and their sages reckon the birds' landing a heavenly sign. So diviners travel for quite long distances to meet the birds when the flocks arrive and follow them for even greater distances when they depart. It is said that the diviners pursue the flocks of birds to discover the enigmatic insights the Spirit World has encoded in their behavior, songs, and flight.

The diviners are not the only ones delighted by the birds' arrival. All the desert people go out to the open country when the first flock appears on the horizon. The sages hurry out before anyone else to greet the migrating community. They head to the wasteland in scattered groups, striding with noble arrogance and preceded by the leader, who walks alone, decked out in his ceremonial regalia. Trailing the nobles are the warriors, also grouped in units. Behind the men come clusters of women, who drag their children after them, wave their babes in the air, and chant cheerful ballads, trilling an epic into their children's ears: "Here are the birds that gave you to me last year; they've come again. Here's the *abil-bil*, the egret, which brought you to me, returning to see you. The birds are your mother. The birds are your father. The birds are your brothers. The birds are your family. The birds have come to visit their child whom they entrusted to me. The birds have come to reclaim their trust. When will you be old enough to accompany the birds? When will you sprout wings so the flock will accept you into the tribe and you can migrate with the birds to the Land of the Birds?"

Tears of longing stream from their eyes; these are the tears of desert mothers who know with a mother's intuition that when an infant is born in a homeland called the desert, no mother will enjoy motherhood long, because the infant whom a bird brings into the desert will inevitably imitate the avian community and leave the nest sooner rather than later. Once he departs, his travels will never end. The mother knows that the desert's legal system is what the Law has established and that it treats the babe in her arms as a bird.[2] Once he ventures off alone, she will never be able to reclaim him. From that moment on, the desert will hold him, and the poor fellow won't return. He will never look back at the tent, at the nest, and his mother will have lost him for good. That's why the mother holds her nursing infant high and throws him into the air the day the birds land. She weeps and croons heartrending songs in honor of this maze, because she knows, with a mother's intuition, that once a son heads off into the desert he is not heading off to life—as all mothers hope—but to a maze; he is heading into a labyrinth, one from which he will never return.

The tribe's celebration starts the night the birds land.

Swarms of girls go out to the open countryside shortly before sunset and form a joyful drum circle, trilling shrilly while women poets sing verses that slay the wasteland's stillness and awaken the rebel demon of ecstasy in the hearts of the Spirit World's inhabitants. Then embarrassed female jinn hide in the farthest caverns while male jinn explode with musical frenzy, delight, and anxiety as they approach the group, camouflaged

2. In the works of Ibrahim al-Koni, the Law is the lost but influential customary law of the Tuareg people—al-Namus.

in human garb, and invade the circle to challenge the tribe's warriors' prowess as dancers. The moon rises, lighting in breasts a new zeal, the rhythm grows more intense, poems wax hotter, and the poets' throats become hoarse, although this huskiness makes their voices even more attractive and agreeable. Then the entire encampment is reeling, and the tribe is afflicted by a mysterious frenzy that has perplexed diviners and that not even specialists in the Law have been able to explain.

The singing ends at dawn, but the inexplicable frenzy lasts for days, endures for a long period, and continues for a time that will never be forgotten.

3

When the birds approach the desert and alight as guests in the encampment, they do not immediately perch on the roofs of the tents and do not land in the beds of the wadis to poke their beaks into furrows in search of worms. Nor do they alight in the spaces between campsites to rummage through trash to scavenge grain, crumbs, or leftovers like the local birds, which don't aspire to homelands of the Unknown and haven't experienced a migratory paradise. Instead, the migratory birds approach the campsites in massive, densely clustered tribes that fly in parallel formations, each trailing a wise leader, who flutters at the front, repeating a pleasant and distinctive refrain that the entire tribe repeats after him as its watchword.

Not far off flap the wings of another tribe that differs in color but heads to the same destination, flying to the same unknown homeland. A leader precedes them, soaring through the empty air, repeating a different tune that distinguishes his tribe from the next. Each melody is a beautiful song when heard alone, and the leaders of these avian tribes must teach their flock this watchword, which the birds must repeat to show that they haven't strayed from the tribe's flight path and still follow the tribe's Law, because any bird that does not belong to a tribe becomes isolated, turns into an outcast and, according to the customary law of the wasteland—the birds' customary law—becomes a solitary, lost creature. Fear of becoming lost, dread of the labyrinth, motivates each bird in the tribe to cling to the tribe's sign, its watchword, its melody. So each bird repeats its tribe's song after the leader. In exactly the same way, a son of the desert repeats his name the first time he goes out to the grazing lands, because his mother has taught him that he will be lost forever if he forgets his name.

This is why the tunes are repeated, why birdcalls overlap, and why there are numerous songs. Then the sweetness of the singing is lost, and the pleasure of the melodies dissipates. Similarly, when girls gather in a circle and each sings her own song at the same time, the musical experience is spoiled and the beautiful melodies become a repulsive hubbub.

Before deciding to land, groups circle over the camps for a long time and then spread through the gullies and pastures. Desert dwellers have noticed that their zeal increases, their hymns grow louder, and their dancing through space becomes more graceful and beautiful during the hours prior to their descent to the earth. The singing of some tribes deteriorates into a fierce squawking, however, and the dancing of some other winged communities becomes a feverish frenzy. Is it because a descent from the sky's kingdom to the earth's gullies is so terrible? Or, is the true secret actually the journey, which wayfarers say provides inveterate travelers with a pleasure that so surpasses in sweetness and allure even the ecstasy of musical enjoyment that travelers want it to continue in perpetuity?

A first bird lands on a tent or in a tree in a gully.

The boys yell with glee, the girls' tongues compete in releasing trills, and the voices of the women poets rise in mournful refrains.

Diviners approach with a fox's wariness and walk round the bird, intoning spells, giving voice to a truth they normally confess only to themselves: "You're no bird, bird. Winged people, you are us. Your Law is migratory. Our Law is nomadic. You beat your wings in the sky; we pad over the earth on two feet. You migrate to the nations of the unknown North; we migrate in search of Waw.[3] You eventually return from the nations of the Unknown, because you haven't found the Unknown Nation among the nations of the unknown North; we eventually return from our quest for Waw, because we discover that there isn't any Waw in the desert homeland. All the same, you don't stop migrating and we don't stop searching. You know that heroism isn't determined by a successful arrival,

---

3. In Tuareg culture, Waw (pronounced "wow"), although the name of some actual locations, refers to a paradise-like lost oasis, which is rediscovered only by a blessed few, especially wayfarers who are not seeking it.

and we realize that the search itself is heroic. So, community of birds, do you know why we celebrate your arrival? Because all of us realize that you are us and we are you, even though we don't admit this to anyone else."

4

But can a being accustomed to exploring space, a being whose homeland has become the sky, endure life in the lowlands? Can creatures born and bred between the heavens and the earth enjoy the earth's lowly realm?

The birds' stay in the encampments does not last long.

After just a few days, the cry bursts forth.

The leader of each tribe adopts the role of herald, flies over the gullies, and soars over the dwellings, crying the secret watchword, stridently repeating the departure song. The members of the tribe snatch up the watchword, and their voices gleefully chant this refrain. The hour is set, and the muster begins. So melodies proliferate, songs multiply, and voices drown each other out till the chant's beauty is lost and the enjoyment fades, because feverish travel punctures rapture and the hour of departure swallows the pleasure of the song. When the first wing flutters, forsaking the desert's soil and rising into the expanse of the morning, this bird's wings, which are bathed and marked with colors, look resplendent. Behind him assembled wings of the same color take flight. The flock swoops into the glowing light but does not shoot off toward the unknown homeland until it has circled over the gullies and soared over the dwellings to say goodbye. During this sorrowful flyby, in the course of this painful farewell, throngs from the caravan trail after the flock. Then sages sob, girls choke back tears, and children weep out loud while diviners pursue the flock to detect the prophecy inherent in its trajectory.

Other migrating flocks rise in quick succession and follow each other into the void, which is harsh, stern, uncaring, and eternal. Their songs fade off in the distance, and the din of their melodies dies away, but the diviners continue to pursue them even after they disappear into the harrowing void, where they become part of it, an expression of the purity of the void, a part of it that fades and dissipates into nothingness.

Once the birds have departed, the camps revert to their former stillness and their lethal tranquility.

The diviners return the next day, bringing the prophecy back to the camp. They enter the leader's tent and closet themselves with the leader for an entire night. When they emerge, they face the people, order the attack drums struck, summon the herald to tour the camps to advise the clans to migrate because a drought is coming, or send for the maidens, who will trill joyfully at news of the floods that the diviners have detected in the birds' conduct.

That day the diviners had also spent the entire previous night alone with the leader. When they met with the people that morning, however, they did not order the drums struck, they did not summon the herald to inform the tribes of a drought, nor did they send for the maidens to trill joyously at the coming deluge they had detected in the flight of the birds.

On that day, when the sages silently left the leader's tent, people could see depression and despair in their eyes and despondency and disappointment in their faces.

I I

THE PROPHECY

But then a man didn't need to have to keep his mind steadily on the ground after sixty-three years. In fact, the ground itself never let a man forget it was there waiting, pulling gently and without no hurry at him between every step, saying, Come on, lay down; I ain't going to hurt you. Jest lay down.

William Faulkner, *The Mansion*, Chapter 18

1

Why do the tribes move about? Why do they traverse an area and head to a more distant one? Do they do this to leave a land threatened by drought and famines in search of a land that promises ample grazing? Do they set forth because they fear the ancient prophecy that warns that remaining in one place for forty days invites servitude to the land? Do they migrate because the Law has said that death on camelback is the destiny reserved exclusively for noble nations? Or do their sages inspire the masses to migrate in search of water and grass even though they actually travel in response to another unknown call they do not disclose even to themselves?

Tribesmen understand that the turbans of the wise conceal many secrets. They know that the leader would not have become a leader, the diviner a diviner, and the sage a member of the council of noble elders if this leader, diviner, or sage had not withheld some secret, because anyone who is so tyrannized by his tongue that he fails to keep a secret isn't granted wisdom or authority over other creatures. For this reason, tribes respond to the diviner's prophecy, yield to the advice of the sage, and obey the leader's order. Then they set forth in groups behind any caravan the leader allows to depart and halt when the leader orders them to.

But the tribesmen also know that misfortune awaits tribes if the age frowns on them and discord enters the council of the wise or if disorder finds its way into the leader's tent.

2

When the tribes of the sky disappear into the sky's labyrinth, they leave behind them stillness, despair, and sad, miserable birds that are too ill, wounded, or old and infirm to continue the migration and follow their tribe.

On this most recent journey, the departing celestial tribe left behind an aged crane. Nobody noticed him the first day, perhaps because the terrestrial tribe was consumed by the anguish that the birds' disappearance had caused or perhaps because the sorrow that the people of the sky had left behind with the tribe was vaster than the wasteland itself, swallowing the wasteland and concealing all the creatures that moved through it. According to the revealed law of diviners, sorrow blurs vision and actually blinds the eye. It is said that the sorrow the emigrant leaves behind in the hearts of those he quits exceeds the sorrow that the deceased bequeath to their kinsfolk. Sages offer many justifications for this. They say: "Travel and death are both eternal separations, but we can erect awe-inspiring monuments for our dead, stone tombs that we visit during festivals and that we sleep on by night to gain prophecies, which warn us against an enemy, an epidemic, or a drought. Moreover, when the jinn become unruly and upset us, we go to these tombs, dig up their stones, and remove the bones of our dead to use for talismans we carry on our travels and employ to ward off the people of the Spirit World. Family members who leave to take a distant trip, however, vanish. We cannot find their burial places or locate any trace of them."

There is, however, another cause for the painful sorrow with which desert tribes normally say farewell to travelers. This is an obscure reason that tribes sense but do not understand. Sages know it but persistently conceal it from themselves. A confused, murky token whispers in their breasts with a murmur like wind rustling. It says that only the wayfarer is promised entry to Waw, that only the traveler can locate the errant continent, and that only a traveler dandles in his heart the hope of reaching the lost oasis. All the same, the traveler is ignoble, conceals his hope by compartmentalizing it, and tries to convince himself that there is no hope, because he knows that if he does not conceal this hope from his ego, it will conquer him and he will tell someone about his hope. Once the tongue utters the secret, the secret is ruined and the treasure—the gold dust—will turn to ashes. But the people seeing off the traveler are also ignoble, because they guess the truth and detect the traveler's intent in his eye before they learn it from a slip of his tongue. Then temptation incinerates them, their breasts flare with longing, and envy torments them. So they weep. They weep not from sorrow about this separation but about the idea that a misguided, errant creature just like them—a wretch like any of them, someone who, like them, has never known whence he came or where he is heading—will find the track they haven't and will be guided by the Unknown to the oasis that the desert's inhabitants have been promised since they first came to the desert. Then he will never again know the suffering of this excruciating quest and longing's pain will vanish from his heart, because the forgetfulness that Waw affords him is a panacea for the world's ills. Then the equilibrium of things is reestablished, and the traveler, whom the wasteland has threatened with its labyrinth, becomes a newborn while the community that said farewell to him and that considered itself safe on account of its sedentary life becomes a desperate, wretched, lost people. When they weep, they do not weep for the newly lost traveler, even if he was their closest relative, but for themselves because they realize they are lost. Then the emigrant becomes an enemy even if he had once been their dearest friend or even their brother or father.

The birds fly off during the migratory season, and everyone returns to his personal concerns while combating an indecipherable longing, his longing for the Unknown from which he came one day borne on the wings of a bird, because the bird that brought him to the desert when he was an infant wrapped in the swaddling clothes of forgetfulness won't be able to carry him back to the Unknown, to his homeland, now that he has outgrown them.

3

In the morning the children found the venerable bird squatting on the ridgeline of a tent. The kids discovered him after the grown-ups had departed to attend to adult affairs. Then the boys surrounded the dwelling and debated how best to reach him. One fetched a long pole and beat on the corner of the tent to frighten their guest, but the haughty bird remained huddled there, holding his long neck back, shielding his head with his wings, and then extending his red beak into the air. He opened his eyelids entreatingly, revealing an anxious eye. A tall, scrawny lad picked up a stone, which he lobbed toward the bird. It rolled over the haircloth fabric and down the tent's other side. Then some boys started yelling, waving their fists in the scrawny youth's face.

"This is a sin. It's like hitting your mother or father. Would you throw a rock at your mother? If the adults see you, you'll be punished."

A boy, whose head sported a Mohawk that resembled a hoopoe's crest, jumped from the pack and warned, "Keep away! He's my guest. Don't you see that he chose our home, not any other? I knew he would come 'cause I've seen him in a dream three times. He brought me good news! The grown-ups say birds bring good news."

The tall, lanky boy with the pole mocked him. "Good news? Don't you see he's old? Old birds bring bad luck, not good news."

"How do you know he's old, sourpuss?"

"Just look at him. Can't you see he's old?"

"Perhaps he's tired. Don't forget he's come from a distant land."

"If he weren't old, he wouldn't have stayed behind when his flock left."

"Perhaps he's ill or wounded. I don't see anything that shows he's old. Guys, do you?"

The children yelled, but the thin boy's voice rang out once more. "The bird's old, and old birds bring bad luck. Drive the ill-omened, old bird away if you don't want misfortune to strike your house."

The boy with the Mohawk lost his temper and shouted, "You talk this way 'cause you're jealous. You're a bad, hateful boy and talk that way 'cause you're jealous."

But the thin boy started to circle the tent, hopping on one foot, and chanted the cruel song that has been passed down from one generation to the next. The boys' ancestors supposedly sang it over the heads of the elderly, who were thrown into pits, where they were left to their fate.

Wiggegh temmedrit atgeed ad tedwelad.
Wiggegh torna atgged at tezied.[4]
You're not a child we're waiting to see grow up.
You're not a sick man we're waiting to see recover.

A group of boys answered this call and chanted the cruel refrain, dancing along behind the thin lad. The other group stood frozen, glancing back and forth between their naughty playmates and the bird that crouched on the tent. Many of them expected to see him recoil and shrink back as the racket made by the boys reached a crescendo and their voices grew even louder to match the agonizing rhythm.

4

Around noon the bird twitched, edged up a little higher, and spread out his right wing and right leg as if stretching. Then he unfolded his left wing and held it extended over his left leg for a time. He pulled himself

---

4. In Tamasheq in the original Arabic.

erect and straightened his very tall frame—his scrawny body supported by two even scrawnier legs. His long beak, which was thrust forward, was longer than his legs.

In the crowd of boys, a voice exclaimed, "This isn't an *abil-bil*."

The boy whose tent the bird had chosen retorted: "Are you adult enough to know all the kinds of birds?"

Another voice called out, "He's right. This is some other bird, an unknown species."

The tall, lanky boy intervened, "Whether he's an *abil-bil* or some other bird, he's certainly old, and old birds bring bad luck to camps."

The bird flapped his wings and beat the air listlessly and desperately. He held his wings extended for a moment and then emitted a strange cry, a muffled squawk, before fluttering his wings and attempting to fly. He rose barely a foot into the air with a ponderousness, slowness, and awkwardness that did not match his meager body. He fluttered his wings with all the ponderousness, slowness, and awkwardness of chickens that rebel heroically against their nature, experiment with disavowing their origins, and take flight, becoming callow citizens of the heavens.

The bird headed toward Retem Valley, covering some distance. Then he fell, descending to the earth like a chicken. He fell ignominiously, in a manner ill-befitting a bird. He plummeted but never stopped beating the air with his large wings, which were lustrous but marked by feebleness and blackness. He touched the ground with his feet, and his toes scratched grooves into the earth for a long distance. The children pursued him, and he ran clumsily from them like a crow. He ran as if favoring his right leg and the left one as well. When the boys closed in on him, he rose again some inches into the air before falling back to earth. He landed in an embarrassing way, and his noble beak sank into the dirt. He wrested it from the furrow, from disgrace, and beat the air with it to shake off the dust and humiliation. In his tired, languid eyes the boys saw the gleam and moisture of tears.

Then the lanky lad said meanly, "Didn't I tell you he's old?"

5

The sun was starting to set, and shadows were stretching toward the East. The North was liberal with moist breezes, and the heat's scattered remnants were retreating with the passing of the siesta hour. So people were emerging from their tents, and the nobles sought refuge in the shade of their homes to debate, wrangle, and enjoy the evening shade and the Northern breezes.

The leader also resorted to the shade of the tent.

He sat on an old leather mat that time's tongue had licked, stripping it of all its hair. He began to amuse himself. In his lap he placed a piece of barley bread, which he started to crumble in his hands, throwing morsels to the bird, which proceeded to bend over these crumbs, languidly and nonchalantly plucking up bits, as if eating not because he was hungry but because he too wanted to amuse himself. The leader murmured, "You're really old. You're so old that your advanced age was obvious even to the youngsters." The leader had rescued the elderly bird from the hands of those wretches some days earlier. He had gone to Retem Valley at noon and found the bird running in a ridiculous fashion, desperately fluttering in an attempt to liberate itself from the earth, from the burden of the earth, from the sovereignty of the earth—but to no avail! Creatures when they become senile, when they grow old and become weak and incapacitated, find the earth waiting for them, find that the earth is their destiny, that the earth is their eternal homeland, their last resort, even if these creatures are celestial beings, even if these creatures are one of the sky's communities like the birds! If the earth weren't so greedy, if the earth weren't so ignoble, if the earth weren't so wise, it wouldn't have been able to find on its surface any dust from which to create creatures. What is the dust of the earth if not the bones of past creatures and the graves of the dead who in antiquity became food for the earth? How can this wise mother create a being that strives if she does not sustain herself? In ancient times, didn't the people of the desert produce the body of the desert? This is the sign. The senile bird was a sign. An aged being weighs heavily on the earth, because she attracts him, pulling him to her. She tells him, "Your return is approaching. The time when you are destined to return to my belly is nigh. I have lavished food on you while you were alive. Today you must draw near and prepare to provide nourishment for those who come after you." The creature is afflicted with terror. The bird was afflicted with terror, because he sensed an unaccustomed weakness and a mysterious force that was drawing him to the lowest possible level. His wings betrayed him, his body failed him, and the sky drew farther away from him, because he did not know that the sky itself, his homeland the sky, was also incapable of changing a single symbol in destiny's Law. It had handed him over to destiny, which was ramming him downward, executing the harsh dictate to return him to the earth.

He heard the youngsters discussing old age, using the word "*amghar*" more than once,[5] and did not know whether they were talking about the bird or him.

6

The diviner approached, and they discussed, again, the beauty of old age and the nobility latent in every sorrow.

The diviner squatted down beside the leader and pursued the mirage into the wasteland, following it till it swallowed the horizon and turned into tongues of diaphanous flame. He picked up a pebble and threw it toward the bird. Then he, as he usually did, made straight for his point from the farthest reaches of the earth. "I've never seen another bird so tame around people from day one."

The leader tossed out some scraps of barley bread, but the bird felt dispirited and became increasingly downcast. He cowered and gazed at the bread crumbs without any interest. Then he closed his eyes and hid his head between his wings. The leader said, "He was forced to act this way against his will. He acts tame because he is alone, deserted, and lost—lost like us. Moreover, don't forget that he's old. The secret lies in his advanced age. Old age is ugly. Does the Law discuss anything uglier than old age?"

The diviner smiled. He circled the topic and hovered around the point, although he continued to explore the ends of the earth. "I fear that what the Law says about old age disagrees with my master's statement."

"I know you will lead me to the ancient kingdom to tell me about the beauty of sorrow once again. Or am I wrong?"

"You're right, Master. But I don't derive my views about old age and sorrow only from the satchel of the Law. Our forefathers were the first to pass down this maxim. It is the forefathers who said that the sorrow of old age is noble and that there's nothing more beautiful in the desert than a sorrowful person. Didn't my master disapprove of the guffaws of the

---

5. Tamasheq for shaykh, old man, leader, or grandfather.

masses? Didn't my master expel Ababa from the council a few days ago when an audible laugh escaped from him? Did my master do that out of respect for the Law of Dignity or from fear of the Law of Wisdom?"

"But don't you consider the sorrow you discuss to be the end's shadow? Don't you think it is death's specter?"

"If it weren't the end's shadow, we wouldn't discover in it beauty's shadow. If it weren't death's specter, we wouldn't see in it nobility's specter. The secret is always in death."

"Why do desert people sing the praises of the end? Why did the forefathers bequeath to us a complete Law in praise of death?"

"Because they, Master, learned from experience that there is nothing so worthy of worship as death. They worshiped it not because it is the desert's only truth and not because it is the only antidote with which they treated the ills of yearning and the pains of the desert, but the secret, Master, is in their longing for the secret, because death is a secret, and they longed for nothing so much as they longed for the secret."

The leader tossed out some crumbs and shook off his lap. He followed the effusion of the mirage in the wasteland. He said, "Do you mean they worshiped death, wishing for death, because it would disclose to them the secret of the Spirit World?"

"Now my master is drawing close to the secret."

"But how would it help them to discover the secret after it was too late?"

"The truth, Master, the truth! Truth is the consolation."

"Don't you think it stupid for man to seek death so he can know for certain that beyond the gloom he will meet a god?"

"Do you want them to be satisfied with life in these dead boundaries? Isn't that more heroic than life in the boundaries of the mute desert?"

"I want them to be satisfied with what they've been granted. I want them to be satisfied with life within the boundaries of life."

"Does my master want a life without truth?"

"Why do you all persist in looking for truth in the Spirit World?"

"Because, Master, that's the only place that truth exists. The only truth, Master, is in the Spirit World."

"How harsh that is!"

The leader picked up a pebble and muttered, "How harsh that is." Throwing the pebble aside, he continued, "Let's return to the bird. I heard the lads say he doesn't belong to the tribe of *abil-bil* birds."

The diviner descended from his heights and approached the source. From his pocket he drew snares to bag the point. "Whether the bird is an *abil-bil* or another similar species, according to the Law it is a messenger."

The leader fell silent. So the diviner continued setting his traps. "The birds have begun to migrate. Since this bird refused to migrate, that is a bad omen, Master."

The leader's eye gleamed with a smile. Did the leader smile because he had discovered the site of the trap? Did he smile because he had realized that the sole reason for the diviner's visit was to continue the previous day's discussion about the need to migrate? He asked, "How can you expect him to migrate when he's old? How can you expect him to fly when the earth has tethered him with chains and his wings are broken?"

"The bird is a migratory creature, and a migratory creature must migrate, even if he is old, because he will contravene his nature and contravene the law of things if he doesn't. Migration is his destiny, Master."

"But old age cripples the body, addles the mind, and tethers the poor creature to the earth with iron chains. So how can it explore the sky and join the celestial caravan? Search your Law for another path for it; don't ask the poor creature to oppose the will of our mother, the desert."

The diviner took another step closer to the site and struck his hands together. He said, "O God of the desert! Does my master think that the bird is this senile? Doesn't my master see that the bird has refused to fly not because he can't fly but because he is carrying a prophecy to the encampment?"

Their eyes met. The two men faced off at the mysterious site. They circled round the source that is the only destination for the community of diviners when they embark on their quests. It is a shadowy spring, a melancholy source they refer to in their arcane jargon as a sign.

The diviner saw that the leader had discovered the site and shouted, "Old age is truly a noble homeland, Master, but it's an ailment that does not yet threaten my master's body."

The leader turned his eyes far away. He smiled and returned to the wasteland, to the playful mirage in the wasteland. He smiled for a long time. He smiled because he had discovered the diviner's secret, his secret reason for visiting. He had known the diviner would arrive shortly. He had known the diviner would come as a messenger from the Council of Wisdom. He had known that they would not let the matter drop easily. He had known that they would come to him individually and in groups, evenings and nights. He had known that they would not oppose him on any matter, but also that they would not yield easily, especially when the matter related to a dictate of the Law, especially when the matter related to a practice that had helped mold them since they were born and had become a religion for them, especially when the matter related to migration. He had excused them, understanding that they were right to struggle desperately to obey a command they had inherited from their grandfathers and had read in their laws, a dictate that had coursed through their blood till it became their life. But he knew as well that they did not know in which land he stood, in which desert he had found himself during recent years, and what it means for a man to discover overnight that everything he has done in life is lost, that everything he should not have done is what he has done in life, and that what he has not done, he will never be able to do, because his time is disappearing faster than he expected, what he thought was life, what he had depended on, had ended before it began, had ended at the time he had planned to begin, indeed, even before he planned to begin. He was discovering that life had passed in the hour he was preparing to begin life—what trivial people call life. Now they wanted him to move about like in the old days. They wanted him to stock up on poems of longing, to set his sights on the stern, shadowy, indifferent horizon and rush off, to dart away toward the horizon in search of what lay beyond the horizon, to hurry off toward the horizon in search of the lost oasis that he knew he would never find. He was duty-bound to hope it existed if he wanted to continue playing, because this was the basis of the game. Whenever the horizon disclosed a void—an expanse, another horizon even less forgiving, even more murky, even more cunningly indifferent—he fought back the lump in his throat, cursed Wantahet both privately and publicly,[6] and diverted himself with songs of grief, because the nomad contents himself with the Waw he finds in poetry once he discovers that this perfect oasis does not exist on earth. But old age mocks every deception and sees what all nomads fail to see. It sees what the diviner does not see. It sees what the Law itself does not see. This is the secret of old age. This is the secret of the sorrow that the diviner saw in the old man's eye and called beautiful.

_____

6. The Jenny Master, a trickster figure in Tuareg lore and a passionate advocate for nomadism and for the she-ass—not the camel.

III

THE DEPARTURE

Nature likes continual creation and continual destruction, because nature is not fit to create anything that can be depended on.

Arthur Schopenhauer, *The World as Will and Representation*

1

But they did not know his secret; they did not understand why he contended with the rugged terrain every day to descend to Retem Valley. They did not know why he isolated himself there from morning to noon. They did not know because they had not heard the song; they had not been delighted by the Unknown's anthem that hid in the groves of retem trees. If they had known, if they had heard, they would have realized that the leader would not reject being uprooted, would not refuse to order the people to move on and separate from their mother, the earth, merely because old age was drawing him to this place the way that the bird from the flock was drawn to the earth of the encampment. If they had heard, they would have realized that the leader would never have contravened the Law of past generations even if feebleness bound him with the strongest chains of iron. If they had heard, they would have realized that the matter involved a secret greater than decrepitude, stronger than a feeling of feebleness, and more profound than the disappointment with which anyone who reaches an advanced age and discovers that the path that previously swallowed his ancestors is the same abyss, the same gloom, and the same forgetfulness that awaits him.

He heard it for the first time a few days after they arrived in this land. He descended into the virgin valley, where the bottomlands were covered with a band of smooth sand marked by attractive folds reminiscent of the earliest days of creation when the original grandfather left his kingdom and ventured into the wasteland for the first time. Into this sandy expanse retem trees had raced each other, but rocky borders had crowded them out of the adjoining tract, depositing in the areas at the foot of the mountains swords cloaked with polished stones that time's torrents had burnished till they gleamed in the sun's rays. Trees had found no place to expand there. So they had turned back on themselves, massed together, and created in the valley bottom thick groves reminiscent of date palms in oases when they encircle springs of water, interlace, cohere, and cluster together as if to hide the spring from inquiring eyes, as if hiding the spring from people for fear they will envy this treasure. To the crest of upper branches of these groves come birds, doves, to build splendid nests. They lay eggs in the nests, sit on those eggs, and sing their monotonous melodies during the siesta hour.

In the retem grove he heard the bird's song as well.

Unlike the doves' songs, it wasn't at all monotonous. Unlike the doves' songs, it wasn't monotone or monochrome. Unlike the doves' songs, it wasn't boring.

In this song, the bird's voice modulated, there were multiple rhythms, parts rose and fell, the lament grew ever more intense, and the tune became purer and mixed with the wail of the wind in the crests of the retem trees, altering the ballad. Then the breeze died down and the *lamento* calmed, but the sorrowful sweetness, the sweet sorrow, never left the song. Indeed, the tune became more sorrowful and increasingly sweet and delightful. Then all the jinn in his breast awoke. They listened, reveled, and entered ecstatic trances, carrying him off through time to return to him what time had taken. They didn't restore to him the harsh, lethal memory that lights a fire in the heart but never brings back what has passed away. Instead they spirited him off to a space where space does not exist. Then he found himself in a time where time does not exist; a space that has not yet become space and a time that has not yet developed into time. So he saw . . . saw what he had always tried to see. He saw what the desert had hidden from him. He saw what time had snatched from him. So he wept. He wept like a child. He wept because only a child sees nothing disgraceful about weeping. He wept because he had retrieved his lost childhood, which he had thought time and old age would never return to him. The bird fell silent, but the man did not return to the valley, to the desert, to space, to time. He remained in the world of the jinn for a period. He stayed suspended in a void devoid of all the characteristics of the void, hovering in space lacking the special qualities of space, soaring in a time that gave birth to no one and that swallowed no one, because it was a time that had not yet been born.

The bird fell silent, and stillness settled over the valley—the ancient stillness, the mysterious stillness, the hostile stillness, the lethal stillness, which declares in its mute tongue that the homeland that knows no spatial borders and that isn't delimited by time is the only homeland for living beings, the homeland appropriate for living beings and for life, because it is a homeland that lies outside life. Why would a creature who one day visits that homeland and then finds himself put back in the cage bounded by feebleness, disability, and old age not weep? Why would the creature who has visited the homeland, to whom the Spirit World has been disclosed, not weep when he finds himself confronted by the eternal, stern, naked wasteland flooded by the mirage's streaming tails?

2

Forty years ago they tracked him down in the distant grazing lands.

They came to him after he had been gone for some months.

He was afflicted by angst—a curse said to be especially common among poets—and went to the borders of the Western Hammada to find solitude as desert dwellers do when they suddenly discover that they have been afflicted by an incurable disease. But they did not grant him any respite. The elders did not cut him any slack. They came looking for him just days after the leader passed away. They told him that he was the deceased leader's only sororal nephew and that he was therefore duty-bound to assume the tribe's leadership. He argued with them. That day he debated with them. He was still young; so he argued with them. He told them he was a poet. He told them he was not merely a poet but an afflicted poet. When Emmamma asked what he meant by "afflicted," he said naively that he was afflicted by a disease called sorrow. Then all the noble elders began to laugh. They shed their grave demeanor and all laughed together. He heard the elders laugh out loud for the first time. He was stunned that these sages would violate their eternal Law and guffaw in response to a statement that he thought wasn't very amusing. He thought that they were perhaps laughing for some other, secret reason—not in response to his reply.

They immediately plunged their fists into the dirt to ward off the evil that their laughter might have aroused. They asked forgiveness from the god of the desert, vowing to slaughter a sheep when they returned to their encampment as a sacrifice to expiate the sin of laughter. Then . . . then they adjusted their veils over their faces, carefully concealing their noses, and brought themselves back into conformity with the Law.

Emmamma asked, "Do you want us to violate a tradition that no one in our community has ever violated?"

"The leader has sons brighter than I am and wiser than most men. Why shouldn't they inherit the post of leader from their father?"

Asaruf shouted, "Do you want us to pass the drum to sons of a departed leader who leaves a sister's son in the tribe? Do you want us to violate our forefathers' decree—which we have inherited—carved on the tablets of the lost Law?"

"But I'm a poet, and poets have never made suitable leaders."

Ejabbaran spoke up for the first time. Throughout this discussion he had been raking the dirt with his finger, tracing letters of their ancient alphabet. He didn't reveal their meaning, however, because this wise old man erased these symbols before they spelled out a word. He was bent over his symbols when he observed, "Becoming leader won't prevent you from reciting poetry, Master."

Yes, the sage Ejabbaran was the first person to utter this sacred term of address. He was the first person to place the blue band on the youth's turban and to drop the executive drum, the war drum, before the dead leader's nephew by using this word, which doesn't take up much space in the language's lexicon but which is the final word among desert tribes.

Silence reigned, but the sage continued to trace letters of the alphabet in the dirt, erasing what he had written before the words were complete enough to be read.

He heard Emmamma suggest, "Yes, our sage has spoken correctly: you can recite poetry in secret."

"I should recite poetry in secret?"

"Yes, you can recite your poems in secret the way the tribe's elders do, just like all the leaders."

"Like all the leaders?"

"Yes. Do you think you're the only desert leader who enjoys reciting poetry? Know that all leaders in the desert are poets."

"I have never heard a leader recite a poem."

"You haven't heard a leader recite poetry, because they recite in secret, as I told you. They recite their poems in secret, attributing them to female poets or foreigners."

"But does poetry remain poetry if a man recites it in secret? Does poetry remain poetry if the reciter attributes it to someone else?"

Ejabbaran spoke again, "This is what we found our fathers doing, Master."

He hunched over the dirt, lost in his letters, drawing and then erasing what he had drawn. He would write a symbol and erase it. He seemed to be immersed in his world rather than present with them.

This is what made him feel that the expression "Master" was decisive when Ejabbaran uttered it; it seemed that the Unknown had uttered it.

3

Not many years passed before they came to him again.

Water had cascaded down the valleys, and many meteor showers had lit up the sky. The tribes' poets had recited splendid new poems, and the maidens had sung heartrending ballads. Elders had dozed off, and the tribes had lost wise leaders. Then the elders came to their leaders' sisters' sons to place the blue cloth band on their heads, to hail them with the title "Master," which previously had been said to him in the wilderness when he was named the tribe's leader. Then they came to him again, just as they had come to him in the deserts of the Western Hammada. Emmamma led them as he had on that day, but wise Ejabbaran was unable to come, because this ancient sage had ceased tracing his symbols in the desert's dirt and lay in an awe-inspiring tomb beside his ancient ancestors.

The sage was absent this time, but Asaruf came with Emmamma. The leader observed how one messenger's head would be higher than the other's only to be outstripped by his partner's by a turban's height. Then the first man's head would gain the ascendency once more, rising above his companion's by the same distance. He remembered that this noble situation—when companions the same height alternately appear taller than each other on account of their gait, as if they were competing to climb heavenwards—is known in poetics as "Amisarrasan."[7]

They came in the evening. They didn't track him down in the wasteland of the Western Hammada as they had once done. They came to him in the dwelling they had selected for him long ago. They came to him, and he realized at once why they had come. He perceived that secret today with the mind of a leader, the mind of time, which was gushing past with the torrents in the valleys, vanishing like the early afternoon mirages, and carrying away his whole life. He perceived today the secret he had not perceived that day when he employed a poet's intuition, that noble insight, which is tender and delightful and which they had come that day to seize from him. They had stifled it in his breast forever. They

---

7. Disproportionate, dissimilar.

had stifled the poetry in his heart on that ill-omened day. Then he himself had smothered. He had kept trying to breathe, gasping for air, hoping to bring back his lost bird. He had been wheezing all this time, breathing laboriously with a distressing sound—like someone wailing and trying not to weep—because when a man suffocates, he finds no way to draw in air; all he can do is weep. The eternal desire to breathe, to reclaim his lost bird, caused him to forget the ceremonies preordained for him and to ignore the law of leadership. He committed another error, one the elders thought inappropriate for a leader. So they contacted each other, consulted with each other, reached a decision, and came to him. He knew what they would say on this occasion. Time had truly taken his life but in exchange had granted him a small talisman, which the Law called by many names: experience, intellect, and wisdom. By means of this talisman he was able to decipher the prophecy. Yes—they would say, "This is inappropriate." They would say that the leader's life was the tribe's life and that it was inappropriate for the leader to be married to a poet now that he had reached a mature age. They would say that the leader's destiny was to sacrifice himself in order to improve the tribe's fate, to sacrifice happiness just as he had previously sacrificed his solitude and poetry one day. They would say that a man who enters the tent of leadership must forget about love, just as he had previously forgotten solitude and poetry. In the leader's tent there was no room for any fantasy, and love is a fantasy. Love is a great fantasy; love is the greatest fantasy.

He would argue with them; he wouldn't remain silent. He would debate heroically with them, with all the heroism of a lone man, a defenseless man ambushed by enemies armed with the most vicious spears. He would tell them that they had stifled in him the noblest of breaths one day. They had slain his first beloved in his heart and today, decades later, had come to slay heaven's gift in his heart, to take from him his last consolation, the last amulet that heaven had provided him before snatching everything from this wayfarer. In the past they had taken everything from him. How would it harm them if today they allowed him to keep his little doll, if they let him retain a wife who recited poetry after they had forbidden him to recite it? What harm would it do them to leave near him an unassuming creature who sang lyrics to him during melancholy moments to make up for the songs they had stolen from him one day? But could he convince them using such language? Would the logic of a child from whom they had taken a doll suffice to convince intellectuals? Could someone who had filled his heart with the Law's sternest dictates understand a poet whose tongue had been removed? Would wisdom's heroes, the arrogant advocates of severe scriptures, understand the language of a wounded lover?

Yes, he lost the argument that day, too. That day he failed as well to convince the eternal clique, the stern clique that no longer recognized poetry after trading it in for the provisos of the Law, the clique that lost the secrets of passion when it embraced a religion called "Concern for the Tribe's Destiny." So they were disappointed to find him speaking a language they thought he had forgotten long ago, one they deemed inappropriate for His Honor the Leader. So they defeated him. They vanquished him. When they left, all he could do was sob with grief, suffocating from the calamity, because calamity had become his default consolation during the decades he had spent alone.

4

After this defeat, he wrote his beloved a note saying that leadership was a curse he had not chosen, that destiny alone, so it would seem, was what had decided his fate by making him the late leader's sister's only son and that he had not been able to rebel against the will of the elders back then, long ago, because that would have meant not only a rebellion against the elders but a desperate contravention of destiny's volition. This passionate woman, however, didn't recognize logic's language, didn't understand the secret of destinies, and considered the Law to be a handful of dead words, of deadly words. If his beloved had been just any woman, it would not have been so hard, but she was both a woman and a poet; she wasn't just a poet, but a poet in love. What earthly argument could sway a female poet in love? Before she departed and deserted the tribe forever, she sent him a note too, an angry note, a note in which she said that she had decided to do what he ought to have done. She said that self-imposed exile in the far-off wastelands had in the past been a male prerogative but apparently now the situation had changed, just as everything had changed, because men now were forcing women to choose exile, forcing women to be heroic (because the ultimate expression of heroism is self-imposed exile) while they, men, secluded themselves in their homes. Then he received news of her. They told him she had emigrated; she had migrated to an unknown land. After that no one ever saw her again.

He went out to the open countryside to bury his defeat there. He went to the wasteland to contend with the ancient lump in his throat, to sob over this calamity instead of reciting beautiful poems and chanting sorrowful songs, because the bird of poetry had flown away, becoming lost, and the voice of song had choked and died.

5

And here they were—coming to him again.

They came as they had come long ago in expanses of the Western Hammada. They came as they had once come to take poetry from him, as they had come on another occasion to take his beloved from him, taking the poet from him, leaving him alone and abandoned with no companions save solitude, calamity, and a life that time had decimated, leaving it a fantasy like any other.

Here they were coming again today to confiscate something else, but what was there left to take? Were they a group charged to take, a group that would never lack something to take? Yes. Yes, these elders would never lack for something to take from the leader's dwelling. They arrived one day to take the bird, to take the secret he had hidden in the retem thicket, in the sanctuary's groves, in the valley he had placed off limits to the hoi polloi when he told the herders, vassals, and slaves: "Anyone entering Retem Valley from today on will have his head chopped off with a sword." So everyone had avoided it and had kept their herds out of it. He had stationed mounted warriors on its heights as guards. He had done that as a precaution to erase the evidence, to hide his little secret. Had the jurists discovered this little secret too?

Were they too stingy to allow him this play-pretty? Had they come to deprive him of the bird, the song, and the secret—camouflaging their action with the need to uproot themselves in obedience to the law of nomadism?

When they approached, he went out to meet them in the open. He hurried to greet them out of respect for Emmamma, the same Emmamma, the venerable Emmamma, the immortal figure who had accompanied the elders on that first day in the Western Hammada and who had accompanied the group during the second assault. All the former elders had passed on. Time had carried off Asaruf during the third assault, but Emmamma led the way this time too. He was leaning on an elegant acacia walking stick and shaking. He shook and the stick shook too.

Once they finished their attack on him, he requested just a few days before the forthcoming departure. Emmamma took him aside to say, "Don't think I came because I feared people would say the venerable elder had missed an opportunity to influence the leader concerning some worldly matter, because you know that a person who has turned his back on life will not be much harmed by what is said. I came instead because it isn't a bad omen for the leader to contravene a time-honored law and refuse to migrate; truly the bad omen would be for the venerable elder to fail to join a deputation of elders visiting the leader's home." Then he laughed sorrowfully as he waved his staff before him. He joked, "I have come to you today on three legs. I fear I'll be forced next time to borrow a fourth leg from the acacia tree in order to reach your dwelling."

6

That day, during the few hours that followed the bird's departure, in the brief period after the bird took flight from the groves, rose into the air, and disappeared into space's labyrinth like a speck of dust vanishing into the ocean of the void, at that time when he felt empty and desolate and experienced a distress that surpassed the calamity of the years, that was greater than the pain of his whole life, he dashed out of the sanctuary. He traversed the valley's groves, scaled the rugged, rocky scree with the vigor of a young man, and climbed the elevation leading to the encampment. He took long strides, forgetting that the Law had also stipulated how the leader should walk, forgetting that the forefathers had not neglected to shackle the leader's feet, to teach him to imitate the way cranes walk. He forgot the Law and the forefathers, because he forgot he was a leader. He did not merely forget he was a leader then, he forgot that he was carrying another bird in his right hand. He was carrying the aged bird that old age had prevented from traveling, from joining his close-knit flock. He forgot he had lost that day not only the bird in the groves, the bird that sang, the bird that brought the secret and glad tidings; he had also lost the aged, haughty, indifferent bird that had in recent days been another boon companion for him. Even when he encountered the vassals and ordered them to assemble the nobles for a meeting, he didn't notice their astonishment, he didn't notice that they were looking furtively at his right hand, scrutinizing the dead bird. Even when he approached the sages and met with the elders in the tent, with the immortal Emmamma front and center, he did not relinquish the dead bird. He was still grasping its two long legs and dandling the scrawny body, which death had left even scrawnier and less significant, leaving it the size of a small handful of straw.

When he spoke to them that day, he said, "He left. He departed. He has flown away. You can rejoice: he has departed."

The elders exchanged suspicious glances and looks of amazement and then of disapproval. They did not notice the pallor that had spread over the leader's cheeks because they were following the movement of his long, thin fingers over the bird's body, over its feathers.

The diviner had the audacity to ask, "Who departed, Master?"

He did not reply; instead he continued grooming the bird's feathers with all the affection of a mother combing her virgin daughter's hair on her wedding night. His eyes circled their faces, moving with the ecstasy of someone moved by singing, because he saw what he wasn't observing, because he saw what he had longed to observe for the longest time. He didn't see them. They were all certain that he didn't see them.

He said, "You can make your preparations. You can dodge the horizons as soon as tomorrow. You can flee from here, but realize that you won't be able to flee from your souls. I know you want to flee from your souls, but you attribute that desire to the Law, because you are cowards. Yes, you are cowards. Ha, ha, ha. . . ."

He laughed. The leader laughed. He laughed out loud, actually, offensively.

He didn't just laugh; he borrowed the language of the street and humiliated the council. He characterized them as cowards and denigrated the Law. So was the person sitting opposite them the leader they knew or had the jinn succeeded in possessing him, there in the sanctuary, in Retem Valley, and substituted for him another creature, a hateful member of their jinn community?

The diviner said, "You're feverish, Master. It's best for people with a fever to rest in bed."

The hero Ahallum remarked, "My master is ill. The best thing would be to send for the herbalist."

But a stern sage threatened him with his forefinger. "No, he's crazy. Only madmen speak like this. So send for the sorcerer, not the herbalist."

The leader guffawed again, laughing sarcastically. Then he embraced the dead bird and asked, "What's the point of all this, given that we're setting out tomorrow or perhaps today? Haven't you said that travel is the antidote for every ill? Let's go! Prepare! In fact, rise and depart now. Now! Now! Hee, hee, hee. . . ."

Silence descended over the council, an ancient silence, a mysterious silence, an aloof silence, a hostile silence.

The next morning the diviner appeared before the tribe and made the pronouncement they always feared, the phrase they shied away from just as they shied away from fire—more than they shied away from a raid, more than from an epidemic: "Amghar yazzrenghin: the leader has preceded us."

Children, women, and weak-hearted men began to sob, but the sages yielded to an ancient oasis, to the ancient silence, the stern, hostile, aloof silence.

IV

THE CHAPLET

What is love—this ill-natured thing that makes enemies even of friends?

Vikram Seth, *A Suitable Boy*, 6.24

1

The first garland was plaited like a girl's braids.

He came to her tent shortly before sunset and placed the noble garlands on her lap. She leaned forward to examine the many strands. Then the breath of the mysterious blossoms perfumed her face. She noticed the flowers' slender inflorescences (which young men compared to virgins' locks and avoided referring to as crests) that intertwined in intimate embrace. Two side stems, which were crowned by white flowers with five petals, twisted around a central stem, which was also crowned by white flowers with five petals, the way a snake in the forest twists around the branch of an acacia tree till the branch, in turn, twists around the body of the snake, as the sages of those tribes say. The central stalk, which was crowned by almost imperceptible flowers, borrowed the flexibility of strands of hair to twine around the bodies of the two side stems. Then these slender bodies vanished in this intimate embrace. Of this marriage, all that showed was the soft, tender flowers' fuzz that evoked the essence of a conquered creature. This being curved with the bend of a taut bow, meeting in a part that resembled a bow because in the rigor of the weaving, in the precision of the craftsmanship, in the inchoate, insane desire to suppress the stem, to hide the stalk, and to obliterate the three stems until nothing showed in the braid but retem blossoms, the juncture of the intertwining braids became a noble garland of white pearls.

The creator of this chaplet had not been content to make a single garland; that evening he presented the beauty a whole cluster of them. The beauty inhaled the perfume of the flowers piled in her lap and smiled. She smiled the type of smile that sorcerers normally see only in people "who have spent a long time talking about eternity" (as they describe hermits) and raised her fingers toward the void. The lover saw the row of her lower teeth when she laughed. She laughed in an odd way and then sneezed twice.

Author's Note. Successive generations have affirmed that these events took place before the tribe became sedentary, before the leader's tomb became a peg that tied them to the earth. Even so, some narrators feel that this tale could have occurred in any age and that we may find it playing out in the dwellings of any tribe headed by a leader who is assisted by a diviner.

2

He had settled in the tribe's camp a few months back and had attended the evening parties of the young women in the moonlight. He had, however, not rolled around ecstatically on the ground, and the jinn of ecstatic trancing had not seized hold of him. He had sat off by himself in the open. By sitting apart, he had seemed to be a loner like all foreigners and intimidating like senior jinn. Some individual tribesmen, however, affirmed that they had observed him swaying in response to the music and emitting incoherent sounds in response to the vibration of the single string of the *imzad*, which sought inspiration for its sweet tunes from the stars in the heavens and from the kingdoms of the Unknown. It was, however, certain as well that the ecstatic jinn had not seized him in the young women's circle and that he had not tranced along with other fellows his age.

Suddenly, he stopped attending the full moon parties.

He stopped attending the evening parties and appeared in the grazing lands, where he long kept company with the herdsmen of the lower valleys. Inquiring minds also followed him there and returned to the campsite to say they had heard him sing unfamiliar songs that reminded them of the drone of the jinn in the blue-black mountain caverns. They had been unable to make out the tunes and hadn't understood a single word of his songs. When they questioned the herdsmen about the stranger's conduct, they said he hadn't sung at their soirées and hadn't spoken either. When they had asked him to join in their nightly singing, he had replied that foreigners have a different law and different songs. Since, of all the desert people, herdsmen are the most knowledgeable about the behavior of foreigners, they abandoned and avoided him.

He returned to the tribe.

He returned to the tribe, and then gossips discovered his interest in the poetess.

3

Other people said that his infatuation with her began before he went to the grazing lands, because passionate lovers are wont to seek refuge there.

Fleeing to the wilderness was something everyone did when time struck them with the blow called in the law of love a "blow with the talon." This phrase was borrowed by passionate lovers from the lexicon of sorcery to attribute to themselves. Joining the herdsmen was always just an excuse to forget and an attempt made by everyone smitten by this blow, by this ailment that was the only one sorcerers couldn't treat: love! Meanwhile another group affirmed that the stranger's ailment had not begun until after his return from the homeland where lovers typically buried their lethal ailment. But everyone knows that foreigners are a group who are extremely hard to fathom. Everyone also knows that the stranger's secret would not be a true secret if love's disease did not disclose its nature.

The tribe's stranger also harbored another secret typical of any stranger, but many thought that his true secret had not begun until he became interested in the poetess. So they repeatedly intimated that love actually was his only secret.

Fate arranged for their first meeting to be at one of the nocturnal festivities when the full moon glowed high overhead and its alternative daylight inundated the wasteland. A bird fluttered in the breast then, and people yearned to reach the land of longing. Since they yearned, they sang, because singing is the only wing that can reach the domain of the homeland and enter the realm of the lost dominion. The poet sang with the ancient voice of longing. Then the bird fidgeted in the cage but did not escape. Other throats repeated the song after her, and the bird fluttered some more and beat its wings feverishly to fly off into space. Tears leapt from their eyes, and their breasts were oppressed by a mysterious sorrow. People conscious of the secret tried to vent their emotions by screaming. They shouted until their throats grew hoarse. Then they leapt about, danced, and raced off into the open countryside. But the captive bird attempted to overpower them; so they beat their heads with rocks till their foreheads flowed with blood. They crawled around on their knees and writhed on the ground like madmen. They achieved ecstasy only after a painful journey.

When the party ended, the stranger accompanied the tribe's poet to her tent.

After that, they were frequently observed wandering together in the wasteland and in the valleys near the settlements.

4

She placed the bundle of chaplets in a corner of the tent and hung one luxuriant necklace from the post. She was sneezing, coughing, and struggling with dizziness and a headache. She lay down beneath the tent post, and the garland dangled over her head. It hung down far enough to brush her nose. She closed her eyes, and a smile traveled across her lips—the same indescribable smile that the tribe's sorcerers consider a characteristic of anyone granted the ability to see clearly into eternity.

Her face soon turned red and then pale. She felt she was suffocating and groaned, gasping for air. She raised her slender fingers in the air as she had done when she received the gift, but her palm fell and landed on the ground. She crawled out of the tent and began to vomit loudly.

5

He came to visit her the next evening. He came bearing a new cluster of garlands, which he placed in her lap before sitting down at a distance. He spoke about the desert's intentions and the disposition of the Qibli wind but avoided any discussion of poetry. She struggled with nausea and dizziness and felt short of breath. All the same she continued to toy with the mysterious flower petals while suppressing a mad cough in her chest. When the visitor left, she placed the new cluster atop of the other one, which was piled in a corner of the tent. Then she hung a new garland on the tent post as before, and the fragrance of retem blossoms assailed her. She collapsed and knelt by the post. She felt paralysis spread through her entire body and called out to her slave for help. She asked him to summon the woman diviner.

The diviner lit a fire into which she threw a handful of wormwood and another light-colored piece of something with a foul odor. She said it was an efficacious drug for treating illnesses of the Spirit World. When she saw the questioning look in the beauty's eyes, she explained, "You've inhaled the sweat of jinn. You must avoid loitering in the wasteland at dusk."

6

Neither the handful of wormwood nor the pale-colored piece of something with a foul odor succeeded in curing the malady. In fact, her headache grew worse and she was running a high fever. Strange sores appeared on her body. She began to rave, to sing, and to waste away.

Her friends rushed to her tent and sat near her head. The male diviner was finally summoned. A tall, thin creature approached the tent wearing a somber veil and holding a handful of pebbles. He sat at the entrance of the tent and started to shift the pebbles from his right fist to his left and then back to the right again. The bevy of young women noticed that he leaned over when a pebble fell; he bent down with the concern of someone who has lost a treasure. He searched the dirt and didn't relax till he found that stone. The women present affirmed that there was some secret about this procedure and that the pebbles were some mysterious sorcerer's talisman.

The diviner spoke after a long silence. He clenched his fist around the stones and ordered, "Burn the retem!"

No one understood; her friends exchanged glances. The slaves glanced mockingly at the diviner. But the diviner commanded again, "Burn the retem!"

The questioning looks turned into true astonishment; everyone was dumbfounded. How could these extraordinary garlands woven from retem blossoms be burned? The retem blossom is the splendor of the desert and the favorite flower of all the tribes. Hermits have discerned in its fragrance the exhalations of the lost oasis. Virgins wash themselves with retem blossom water on their wedding nights. Parties are thrown to rejoice at its flowering in the first days of spring; poems are sung by the female poets in honor of its beauty. Heroes and mounted warriors speak of its beauty. What was wrong with the tribe's diviner that he would suspect the retem blossoms and order this sacred body burnt? One of the slaves started to remove the bundles piled in the corner, but the girl leapt from her sick bed and pointed her forefinger at him.

He retreated, but the diviner said, "If you want to be cured, order your slaves to burn the retem and dispatch someone to bring back a scrap of the stranger's clothing!"

Doubt was still apparent in their eyes; the pronouncements of diviners always provoke doubt. The diviner does not recycle statements or advice. The diviner would not be a diviner if he did not invent a statement that no one else had said before. The diviner must say something uncouth.

He put the handful of pebbles in his pocket, rose, and threw out the piles of retem blossoms himself. He left these outside and returned to the tent pole, but the lovesick woman had reached it first and grasped the garland, which she hid in the confines of her flowing *thawb*. She swayed and one of her friends steadied her. Then the poetess lay down on her bed and smiled enigmatically.

The diviner lit a fire and fed the retem blossoms to it. He proclaimed with a gruffness befitting his occupation: "If you all don't bring me a scrap of the stranger's clothing, the girl will die!"

7

What truly baffled the tribe was that when they sent men and women out that night to bring the diviner a scrap from the stranger's clothes, these emissaries found no shred of clothing belonging to him. They searched his residence unannounced and scoured the neighboring valleys where he had often gone to make retem garlands for his beloved. They sent a mounted warrior to the distant pastures and another messenger to the dark mountain caves where he had sought shelter the previous winter. But they found no garment in his dwelling, not even a scrap of linen. In the valleys they found no place where he could have hidden anything, and the mounted warrior returned from the grazing lands empty-handed. From the southern mountains arrived a messenger who said he had found nothing in the caves but the paintings of the first people. The sages felt certain that the stranger was a sorcerer and repeated to one another a clause of the ancient Law: "A secret sleeps in the heart of every stranger. There is always a reason when a son of the desert leaves his own people."

In her tent, the beauty began to expire. The fever intensified, and she experienced difficulty breathing. In the middle of the night she surrendered the most precious gift in life—breath—and began to fade into the distance.

She ebbed away without the enigmatic smile ever leaving her lips.

Her girlfriends said that she had died apparently the happiest person in the world!

8

A throng gathered at the entrance of her tent, and the leader arrived. He surprised the group, and the crowds fell back to make way for him, separating into two lines. He halted in front of the diviner and asked angrily, "What's the meaning of this?"

The diviner did not reply. He bowed and smiled. The leader repeated his question in the same tone. Then the diviner took him by the hand and drew him out into the open countryside. He said, "I wasn't the one, Master, who gave the stranger permission to enjoy a stay in the tribe's encampments."

The leader shouted, "Do you want the tribes to say I violated the Lost Book and expelled a stranger who asked for safe refuge? Yes. I gave the stranger permission to stay with the tribe; I didn't give permission to a sorcerer!"

The diviner replied coldly, "He's not a sorcerer, Master."

"The whole tribe says he is. If he weren't a sorcerer, how could he have spirited the maiden away with sacred retem blossoms?"

"Among some tribes in the forestlands, a young man who loves a girl may kill her."

"Kill her?"

"And if a girl loves a young man, she poisons his food!"

"I won't deny that you know more than anyone else about the tribes of the forestlands, but I've never heard about this hideous tribe before."

"There they think that the lover doesn't win his beloved unless he removes her from the desert!"

"Fetishists! This is the religion of those fetishists!"

"Our stranger fell truly in love with our maiden; so he took her!"

"He took her?"

"Yes, this is the way they talk. They say, 'He took her,' when he has killed her."

He was silent for a moment and then continued, "If you all had brought me a scrap of his clothing, I would have known how to prevent his foul deed. But the clever rogue understood this and was careful not to leave behind any clothing from the very first day."

"I sent riders in pursuit of him. They'll bring him back bound with palm-fiber ropes."

"The riders won't bring him back."

"How can you be so certain?"

"I know this community. They're never caught."

"Is he a human stranger or a jinni from the tribes of the Spirit World?"

The diviner was silent. Then he smiled enigmatically. He rolled a stone with his sandal and said almost in a whisper, "But he will return."

The leader stared at him before remarking, "I see you speak as if this were a certainty."

The diviner limited his response to a nod. Then the leader asked, "Did you read this in the bones of sacrificial animals?"

The diviner shook his turban no. In his lusterless eyes the leader noticed an inchoate sorrow.

With his sandal he too rolled a stone, as if imitating the diviner's gesture. The sun bowed to kiss the stern horizon, which extended like a taut bow, and spilled a profuse purple glow over the wasteland. The diviner followed this glow as it poured forth and washed the pebbles, shrubs, and boulders. He admitted, "I confess, Master: I knew he would do this."

The leader rolled away another stone. He stopped and stared at the void for an instant. As he walked on, the diviner told him, "Master, I heard him say, 'We must dispense with things that we love more than we should.'"

The leader paused and—with the intoxication of the possessed—repeated, "'We must dispense with things that we love more than we should.'" He fell silent, and his silence was matched by the silence of the desert. It seemed that the wasteland thought it should keep quiet and listen too.

In the leader's eyes, the diviner saw the leader's tranquility, a sage's tranquility, a hermit's tranquility. This wasn't normal tranquility; it was something nobler. It was childhood. Yes, the leader wouldn't be a leader if his eyes didn't channel childhood. The sage wouldn't be a sage if his eyes didn't channel childhood. The hermit wouldn't deserve the title of hermit if his eyes didn't channel childhood. Childhood is our lost oasis. Childhood is the oasis we seek. There is no good in an eye devoid of childhood. Do not trust a creature in whose eyes you do not discover childhood.

As though chanting, the leader repeated, "'We must dispense with things that we love more than we should.' How harsh that is!"

He took some steps and clasped his hands behind his back the way a man planning to walk a long distance does. In a different voice he said, "Do you know? I've always tried to say something like this."

The diviner acknowledged, "I have as well, but we never hear what we want to say until others state it for us. This is the secret of wisdom, Master."

"You're right."

The diviner gazed at him and discovered moisture like tears in his eyes.

9

Many wadis flowed with water in the northern desert, many cavaliers courted many virgins before the wadis filled with water, and the women poets recited extremely beautiful poems about love, war, and disgrace.

The tribe discovered that it had stayed in that place longer than it should have, and the sages were of the opinion that they should let this land return to nature. So they ordered the drums struck to signal a migration to the north.

The same night that the drums were struck, the herald made the rounds to alert people concerning what had happened at the tomb. Some individuals had gone to the cemetery at the foot of the hill and found the beauty's tomb empty.

The leader arrived to find the diviner waiting for him. They exchanged enigmatic glances by the light of the full moon. Then they set off for a walk in the open countryside as if by prior arrangement. They didn't speak. They did not speak till they were separated from the tumult of the masses and were certain that the desert had lent an ear and begun to listen.

The diviner began, "Didn't I tell you he'd return?"

"Yes. He disappeared that day as if he was from the Spirit World and returned today as if he was from the Spirit World."

"You don't realize, Master, that he has been waiting. . . ."

"Waiting?"

"Yes. He waited for the dirt to claim its share of the dirt's gift."

"The truth is that I don't understand."

"He waited till the dirt had eaten the flesh, leaving him the bones."

"What will the wretch do with the bones now they have moldered?"

The diviner didn't reply. He didn't stop. He didn't roll a stone with his sandal. He kept walking forward as if he had decided to cross the desert on foot, to migrate, to dispense with everything.

Then he said, "He'll make talismans from them. A talisman for his neck, one for his veil's pleat, one for his left wrist, one for his right wrist, and one for the pommel of his saddle. The talisman is a symbol, and the symbol is the lover's language."

"Did you say 'symbol'?"

Unconsciously the diviner hastened his steps. The diviner knew that the desert is a temptation. The diviner knew that the desert entices people. The diviner knew that going into the desert is a voyage, because the naked continent does not accommodate people who come for sightseeing. Because the only law it recognizes is travel. He outpaced the leader by some distance.

Panting, he said, "The lover knows better than anyone else the misery of destiny, Master. He knows he will never obtain anything, so what matters to him is the symbol. The talisman is the only symbol, Master."

The leader quickened his pace as well. He hastened at a speed inappropriate for a leader, inappropriate for a sage, but didn't feel comfortable calling to ask the diviner to slow down.

The diviner pulled farther away and the distance between them increased, but the leader stumbled stubbornly after him.

In a strange voice he raved, "The symbol. What's important is the symbol."

He studied the horizon, which was flooded by light like daytime. When he realized that the diviner was far ahead of him, he said aloud to himself, "'We must dispense with things that we love more than we should.' How cruel this is; how beautiful this is!"

He repeated the phrase in the wasteland. Then he heard it again like an echo of a mysterious call.

V

THE SUCCESSOR

He is like a witness, isolated from everyone,
but observes the play surreptitiously.

The Upanishads

1

They came that day too.

They came the way they had always come; Emmamma led the way, grasping his polished staff. The diviner walked beside him as he usually did. They came swathed in flowing, lustrous garments accented by bands of blue cloth—the mark of special occasions—one above the veil and the second over the shoulders. They came as they were wont to come whenever the specter of an important affair hovered over the tribe. They came as they were wont to come when the awe-inspiring drum, which was decorated with designs of the ancients, was struck in the leader's tent, when they had contacted each other, assembled, and come in response to the leader's appeal. They came today again while fear circulated and fright was on the prowl in the settlement. Then young warriors, old codgers, women, and children emerged from their dwellings and stood humbly by the entrances to their tents as if waiting for something dreadful to happen or expecting an earthquake. People who have savored a sedentary life and have yielded to the land's temptation also grow accustomed to viewing the noble blue-clad council, which looks black from a distance, as a council of crows and a threat to their sedentary life: a convulsion, a blotting out of indolence, an end to muddling through, and the beginning of every futile deed.

They came today as well, and their arrival frightened the tribe, even though it varied today from those over the past decades. It was different because these elders had before always visited an inhabited residence; today they found the leader's tent vacant.

The immortal Emmamma stopped at the tent's entrance to release a long moan of sorrow, to emit a savage groan of farewell, the groan of a dying man, the distressing groan that ends the life of many people, a groan elders that day heard as a lethal lament. Tears flowed from their eyes, and their hearts bled grievously. The venerable elder swayed like someone in an ecstatic trance. So the diviner supported him on one side and Imaswan on the other.

The aged man rapped the tent pole at the entrance with his burnished stick and shouted, "How many times, House, have we entered to find you inhabited? Today we come and find you vacant?"

He released a moan of lament once more. Imaswan protested, "Noble Grandfather, this isn't appropriate!"

Emmamma wiped the tears from his eyes and from his eyelids, which were lined with rugged wrinkles where tears collected. He retorted, "This is appropriate; this isn't appropriate! This is done; this isn't done! Is this all we know how to say in the tribe's language? Haven't we killed the leader himself with such talk? When he tried to convince us that a poet is ill-suited to serve as leader, didn't we tell him, 'This isn't appropriate'? Didn't we tell him when his heart went pit-a-pat long ago and he wanted to marry the poet, 'This isn't appropriate'? When he wanted to help us and thought we should tarry in a bountiful land, which has nourished and sheltered us, didn't we say, 'This isn't appropriate'? So why shouldn't we admit that we're the ones who killed him with a dagger called 'This isn't appropriate'?"

The diviner said, "It would be better for my master to preside over the council and thus honor the master of the house, because the leader will continue to fret uncomfortably in his new home and won't rest until we finish choosing a successor for the master of this house."

Everyone murmured his agreement. The diviner seated the venerable elder near the tent pole at the center of the assembly and sat down beside him to his right. The venerable elder swayed again and said, "We have sought refuge with you from iniquity, and you have kept us safe. We have appealed to you for judgment, and you have treated us fairly. We have relied on you, and you have fed us. House, where has your master gone? Where has our master vanished?"

He tried to trace some characters on the ground but found he was shaking too hard. He thrust both hands in the dirt (the way sorcerers do when they fear some evil) and sighed. This wasn't merely a sigh; it was another moan, a deep groan that poets use to express painful sorrow and that a sage uses to extinguish anguish: "Hi . . . yi . . . yi . . . yi . . . yeh." Then everyone repeated this moan after him. The noble elders repeated it as if responding to a mysterious call. This emerged from their chests like the groan of a dying person taking his last breath.

2

The sorrow did not dissipate and, beneath the ashes, the glowing ember of pain did not die out. The elders' sense of decorum, however, did not prevent them from yielding to their sorrows for a long time. They substituted for the story of parting the narrative of memorable deeds and replaced chanting with panegyric. They said he had not merely been a leader; he had been a brother to every member of the tribe. They said he had lived like an orphan, lacking family and relatives. To their amazement they hadn't realized, until they lost him, that he had lost his mother and father, his brother and sister, and his friend and consort. They said he had been born alone, had lived alone, and had left the life of the tribe alone. They said he was the only leader in the tribe's history not to have privileged his own opinion, not to have rejected a request from the council, and not to have made a decision without recourse to it. They said in the tribe's history he was the only leader who from the beginning had dedicated his life to the tribe. Even so, the council had been stingy with him about everything, refusing to back down and grant his least request. They commented that his parents had been too stingy to grant him a sister who might have given birth to a nephew to serve as his successor and that they, the council members, had been too stingy to grant him a wife to bear a son to serve as his heir when he lacked a sister's son. They concluded by acknowledging that their misfortune on losing him would be all the greater because they wouldn't be able to find a suitable replacement for his eminence. Emmamma swayed once more; this venerable elder almost led them back to the land they had fled. Then the diviner intervened and told them they should sacrifice an animal on behalf of the deceased man's soul. This suggestion pleased them. They joyously expressed their approval, and the slaves rushed to bring a black goat to the awe-inspiring tomb.

3

They slaughtered the black goat and brought a boy with a thick shock of hair dividing his head in two parts, like a cock's comb. They plunged his hands in the sacrificial offering's blood and dragged him to the tomb, where they placed his hands on its stones. His ten fingers made the sign that had been passed down through the generations. With this sign, recorded in blood, the fingers said, "This is our blood, Master, that has been redeemed by the blood of our son. This is our son's blood, Master, that has been redeemed by the black goat's blood." The noble elders stood nearby and humbly recited this talisman: "This is our blood.

This is our blood. This is our blood." They were silent for a short time. Then they picked up the second talisman. "This is our son's blood. This is our son's blood. This is our son's blood." Then they paused again before competing with each other to recite the final talisman three times as well: "This is the blood of the black goat, our sacrificial offering to you. . . ." Next they knelt, swayed, and sang near the leader's head, the maxim of their forefathers: "Ikrahkay akahal, tamosad akedag. You have become a possession of every time and a sovereign over every place."

They chanted till their eyes swam with tears. Then they sat down to savor the grilled meat and to debate the question of a successor. Imaswan pointed out that tribes normally chose the leader's sister's son as the leader's successor and that if no nephew was available, then the leader's son, and when no son was available, the lot fell to the wisest sage. Emmamma, however, left his homeland, which encompassed all lands because it was the homeland of every space, and liberated himself from the time of every time, because it was the time of all times. He returned to the desert, to the tribe, to the council, and to the meeting near the tomb. With his forefinger he cautioned Imaswan and said in jest, "I see you have jumped to a conclusion. Allow me to correct this maxim for you. The Law states that tribes choose the diviner if the leader leaves behind no nephew or son. The diviner appears in the dictum before the wisest sage. Or, has memory failed me once again, causing me to see what is invisible, hear what is inaudible, and say what is unspoken?"

The diviner smiled and then remarked with a diviner's cunning: "The Law never went beyond sons. The Law left the sages' hands free to choose the successor if the leader lacked sons. In the opinion of other tribes, Anhi washed its hands of the entire affair if the leader lacked a sister's son. Then councils chose a person from outside the leader's family, even if he had sons. With regard to the diviner, all the laws have established that his place is beside the leader, not as the leader. This has been true since the earliest times. Why would our master Emmamma attempt to evade this practice and recite maxims to us from the Lost Book, ones that we have never read or heard of before today?"[8]

The elderly man swayed right and left and stared dejectedly at the diviner, but his was a look that spoke more of the impetuousness of his inner

---

8. Anhi and Lost Book are other ways of referring to al-Namus, the Law.

boy than of old age's fatigue. He asked, "Haven't you heard that the Book said, 'The wisest of the wise,' or has my hearing betrayed me once again? Do you retain such a good opinion of Emmamma, who long ago succumbed to dementia and whose primary homeland years ago became forgetfulness, that you would have him assume charge of the tribe and of you?"

Imaswan replied, "A sage whose homeland has become forgetfulness is easier to bear than idiots who boast about being intellectuals and who—if time should frown and danger lurk—threaten our lives and those of the tribe with their minds."

The hero Ahallum interjected, "Our only option is to allow the Spirit World to guide us by casting lots."

But Emmamma gruffly rebutted him, "No, let's seek the advice of the commander."

More than one voice asked, "The commander?"

Emmamma, who was preparing to return to his homeland, said, "The leader! We must seek the leader's advice."

Glancing at one another, they embraced this idea joyfully and said, "You're right. You're right. Why didn't we think of the leader at the outset?"

4

In the tent, the women sat in a circle around the virgin. They washed her virginal body with precious cologne and rubbed her with salves prepared from retem blossoms. They combed her hair into splendid plaits. Then the older women trilled jubilantly, announcing the good news that she was to become the leader's bride.

They brought her out of the tent at dusk but only reached the hill crowned by the tomb shortly before the sun disappeared. The older women escorted her with their ululations and sad ballads. On the way, the poetess sang verses about yearning, death, and marriage. Her companions repeated the heartrending refrains after her, and then ecstasy seized hold of the young men, who trembled, wept, and leapt out of their dwellings to follow this noble cortege, without daring to draw a single step closer. The procession crossed the level, open space spread with depressing gray stones that had witnessed the fires of their ancient forefathers, because these were piles of more ancient gravestones. Their ancestors had stacked these stones when they cremated their dead. Time, however, had scattered these stones, and the centuries had leveled them with the ground. Then the wind had turned them to their original course, lining them up across the space and arranging them in the wasteland, in the Hammada, which was well endowed with rocks, returning them to their original condition. Save for their color, save for their mysterious darkness, save for the coat of ash cloaking these stones, no one would have realized that this area was the exact location of an awe-inspiring cemetery of the ancients.

When the procession neared the tomb, the women's steps slowed, because the original rites that prescribed the path of the bride to her fiancé's dwelling also prescribed the law for her progress there and decreed that the female should model her departure from her home on the first time a female had set forth resolutely and been spirited away from her father's dwelling to her fiancé's abode. In this way, hesitation became the norm for the bride's procession. The female took one step toward her destiny and one step back out of fear and wariness. She ventured forward, because she knew that it was inevitable that she would set forth one day. She proceeded slowly, dawdled, and felt regretful, because she knew she would never go back. Then she asked the group to assist her with poetry's treasures and to help her in her crisis with sad songs appealing to the fiancé to be kind to his bride. These were songs that encouraged the groom to view his bride as a pitiable creature kidnapped against her wishes from her family's home and that encouraged the bride to play the earth for her spouse, who would represent the sky for her.

The cortege reached the tomb's perimeter, and the council of wise elders sent a messenger to represent them and negotiate with the women. These discussions began in veiled language as the women chanted many demands on behalf of the virgin. Then the envoy would rush back to the council with these before returning to the cortege, saying each time that the groom's spokesmen had pledged to fulfill these demands and that they would even build for the virgin, should she want it, a house located between the earth and the sky.

The women gained courage from this and took a step closer to the tomb and then more steps. Finally the women knelt and wept grievously before they handed over their treasure, placing the bride's hand in the diviner's.

5

The wedding ceremonies ended.

The prophetic rituals commenced.

The crowd dispersed, and the noble elders went their separate ways. Inside the tent that had been erected over the tomb, the diviner sat mumbling secret talismans while clutching the beauty's wrist. He began his instructions in a mysterious voice. "Every woman will find herself wailing in a corner one day while a man holds her wrist. The beauty is luckier than all the other girls because she has been chosen to enter the leader's eternal home."

The young woman's wail grew louder. She muttered softly, "But I'm afraid."

"A young woman has a right to be afraid on entering the house of a man who holds her wrist, because man is the spouse of pain. But what right does the beauty have to be afraid when she sleeps beside a man who has dozed off eternally?"

The girl's wail died away, and her virginal breathing became more regular. In a voice like the wind whispering in the retem groves, she murmured, "I'm afraid of the dark. I'm afraid of being alone. I'm afraid . . . of the tomb!"

"Solitude is a necessary precondition for prophecy, my daughter. Don't forget that you will bring a prophecy back to the tribe tomorrow."

She sighed deeply, as if relieved of a burden, but her wrist continued to tremble in the diviner's hand.

The diviner returned to his instructions. "You will lie down soon and rest your head on the stone of the sanctuary. Have no fear, because I'll be near you. Know that there is no reason for you to fear loneliness or solitude or the Spirit World in a place the diviner frequents. I will be near you, because I am a diviner, and the diviner is destined not to sleep. You will feel drowsy. When you sleep, you will hear a commotion. Don't be afraid then. After the commotion, the bee will come. You will hear the bee buzzing, but don't be afraid. Once this buzzing ceases, our master will arrive immediately. He will come to speak. Listen very carefully to what he says. Listen and remember every word. His remarks may seem strange or cryptic to you or even laughable, but beware: Don't forget or disdain what he says. Don't forget what is said. Don't underrate an expression that may seem devoid of meaning, because words you think lack meaning may be more important than those you find meaningful. So beware!"

The virgin whispered with a virgin's curiosity, "But does my master think that my master will show himself?"

"He may if he feels like it, but what's important is what he says. Remember that the bee's buzzing will precede it. In any event, pay attention!"

6

The diviner arrived at first light and was surprised to find people hovering around the tent. He assumed they were curiosity seekers from the hoi polloi. When he made out the features of the hero, however, he shouted, "I thought only diviners were entitled to stay up nights; reading the news in the hordes of stars is their calling."

The hero jokingly replied, "But my master forgets that the tribes don't wake the diviner when danger threatens the campsite. Instead they rush to the hero's tent."

The diviner inquired anxiously, "Danger?"

"The bride of our master, the leader, has had a mishap."

"A mishap?"

"Her body is feverish, there is a crazed look in her eyes, and her breathing is so labored she seems to be taking a bitter last gasp."

The diviner rushed at the group blocking the tent's entrance. They parted ranks for him. Inside, women were gathered around the girl, and a few old men sat off in a corner. The tent's air was stifling. Foul-smelling, acrid salves mixed with the stench of suspect herbs the old women had squirreled away in their belongings for a long time—the way amulets are tucked away—till they had acquired the musty smell of old bones burning. The only scent he could identify in this upsetting potpourri was wormwood. He felt suffocated by the smoke, and the burning incense made him dizzy. He confronted the women and scolded them loudly, "Stop this! Get this out of here!"

They made a path for him through the group, and he scrutinized the girl. Her face's pallor resembled a corpse's, but her whole body was burning with fever. She was shaking, stretching, and trembling violently. Thick foam oozed from her lips, and trails of saliva ran from her mouth.

Her charming plaits hung loosely down, and her braids had divided into matted little hairs covered with dust.

The women surrounded her. One morose old lady was pressing the girl's body with thin, twiglike hands crisscrossed by many braids of veins. By the girl's head stood another equally stern woman from whose hands dangled a ceramic censer. Long use had marked it and the burning incense had charred it, turning it as black as a piece of coal. Lethal, legendary fragrances emanated from this pottery vessel. The sullen woman went back and forth between the hearth at the entrance and the group of women each time the incense burned out.

He shot a threatening glance at this woman and said in a harsh voice, "Go away!"

The old woman took a step back and replied just as threateningly, "Would the diviner interfere when he knows better than anyone that when morning comes and the bride leaves her husband's tent she becomes the women's responsibility?"

"But the husband whose home the virgin has left isn't just any husband. When the virgin leaves the dwelling of a slumbering leader she becomes the diviner's responsibility, because you know that the fruit of the union in this case is a prophecy, not a child."

"See what the diviner's prophecy has done to the tribe's virgin! She went to seek a prophecy and returned from the Spirit World crazed."

"People like you can become crazed even when loitering in the open countryside—why should you criticize the possession of someone begging for a prophecy from a man who resides in the Spirit World?"

"But she, Master, will die. The girl will soon join the leader and live in the tomb if you don't bring a sorcerer to free her from captivity by the jinn."

"Has she said anything? Anyone who got here before me must repeat every word she said, even if it seems nonsense or idle chatter."

"She has been raving; the poor dear hasn't stopped raving since her first scream woke us."

The diviner leaned over the old woman's head till the end of his turban touched the covers. In a self-controlled voice like a whisper he asked, "What did she say while she was raving? If you collect your wits and remember one statement from what you call raving, I will reward you handsomely."

The old woman's eyes glowed in the firelight. They gleamed mysteriously, and her upper lip, which was a network of wrinkles, rose.

She remarked, "It's really hard to recall a dying person's delirious words, the words of a person who has left the land of games and dolls and reached the far side of the valley."

The diviner drew closer to the old woman's ear and insisted in a voice like a hiss, "In delirium the secret is concealed. In the nonsensical raving of a possessed person is hidden the prophecy."

He whistled and added with all the certainty of a diviner, "In the prattle of a possessed person is hidden the supreme prophecy. So watch out!"

The old woman was silent. She lowered her eyelids, which were also covered with wrinkles. But her hands never stopped massaging the girl's body. Finally she spoke; she spoke without opening her eyes. She spoke like a real diviner: "Tekrahame eddaragh."

She stopped. Her face's wrinkles trembled and its folds expanded. The veins of her slender neck bulged and became a web of veins. She said with the girl's voice, with the voice of prophecy: "Tekrahame eddaragh. Ekaoankrahagh ammutagh. You possessed me when I was alive. Now that I'm dead, I'll possess you."

The diviner repeated numbly, "Tekrahame eddaragh. Ekaoankrahagh ammutagh."

He repeated this prophecy once, twice, several times. Then he straightened himself and lifted his head to look up. As if addressing the heavens he said, "The prophecy! This is the prophecy. We slaughter sacrificial offerings and race off to search for it across the generations, forgetting that it lies between the lips of a possessed person or is hidden in the mouth of a creature we call crazed, for what would become of the desert's tribes if the desert lacked prophecy? What would happen to settlements if the desert lost its leaders and if leaders from the realm of the Spirit World didn't send prophecies via the tongues of possessed people to provide illumination for their tribes' path during the leaders' occultation? Have you finally heard your leader's voice? Isn't this his language? Didn't he always like to speak in riddles?"

He moved to the other corner, where the elders were huddled, and said as though addressing all of them or no one at all—because at that moment he was preoccupied by addressing the tribes of the Unknown, "Isn't what you just heard the wise answer befitting a leader? Hasn't he told you something he wasn't able to tell you while among you? Didn't we possess him while he was alive? Didn't we prevent him from marrying his beloved poet? Didn't we require him to accept the position of leader, which was a shackle for him? Didn't we visit him with groups of people to force him to take trips through the wasteland against his will? Weren't we too stingy to let him enjoy the bird's song? Do you doubt now that the voice we heard is your former leader's? Will you doubt again the power of the dead to carry out a threat? Do you intend to disdain a promise? Or will you heed the advice of wisdom and accept the leadership of a man whom you possessed while he was alive and who has sworn to possess all of you now from behind the curtain? Do you still doubt that your leader will remain your leader forever?"

He turned to the crowd gathered at the tent's entrance and screamed a command: "Slaughter a sacrificial beast! How can a prophecy be taken seriously unless the blood of sacrificial offerings is shed? How do you expect the goddess of this prophecy to recover from the grip of the Spirit World before she's been washed by blood? Bring a black goat if you want the girl to recover. Bring your blackest goats, if you want a real cure that has nothing in common with grannies' nasty incense."

The vassals and slaves rushed off and brought back from the open country the blackest goats. They handed the diviner a bronze dagger. The diviner rushed at the cluster of women and ordered that the sacrificial offering be flung beside the body of the possessed woman. He recited ancient talismans of which no one ever understood a single word. Passing generations had labeled these "arcane" because of their age. They were said to be puzzling because they had been written in the first language, which had become obsolete, vanished, and been forgotten, bequeathing to the tribes only some mystifying words spoken as talismans that not even the diviner himself understood.

He drew the dagger from the scabbard, which was also adorned with talismans. The dagger's blade shone in the firelight and its path traced a design in the void. The soothsayer brought the thirsty blade down on the victim's throat, and blood gushed out copiously. The animal emitted a death rattle and choked with the pains of its dying gasp. More blood flowed from its throat. The blood splattered and stained the maiden's throat, nape, and face. Her body underwent a transformation. The overstressed frame began to relax, the tension left her facial muscles, the possessed look left her eyes, the foam ceased oozing from her mouth, and her breathing became more regular and regained its lost harmony.

A profound stillness settled over the miserable body, and her lips muttered in a sleepy daze, "Tekrahame eddaragh. Ekaoankrahagh ammutagh."

Outside the tent, in the arc of the Eastern horizon, a newborn firebrand appeared, signaling the birth of a new dawn. The diviner muttered, "You're right. Like any other people, we understand nothing about our situation; but we do know that truly no one is better suited to succeed the leader than the leader himself."

VI

THE LOVER

What you sow does not come to life unless it dies.

The First Letter of Paul to the Corinthians, 15:36

The stone expresses that side of the self that rises,
isolated, stretched toward nature.

C. G. Jung, "The Spirit Mercurius"

1

They convened a new assembly, and the diviner began, "Who but the leader can succeed the leader?"

When his question was met with general silence, he posed this challenge: "Let anyone who can bring the tribe a leader fit to succeed the leader speak up."

No one spoke.

The diviner announced: "We repudiated his leadership qualities when he was leader. Now after moving to the Spirit World he has nominated himself as our leader. Should we spurn the Spirit World and ignore the prophecy?"

He pointed his finger at the stones of the tomb and declared sternly, "From today forward, this pile of stones is our treasure. Do you know how he answered me when I asked him about migrations?"

Their curiosity got the better of their sense of decorum, their wisdom failed to buttress their feigned indifference, and their pride lost its ancient, contentious scorn for worldly matters. So at the same time their tongues all blurted out: "What did he say? Tell us—how did he reply to the question about migration?"

The diviner smiled with the malice of cunning strategists and deliberately took his time in replying. He deliberately delayed his response in order to kindle in their breasts the fire of curiosity and to inflame the hearts of the elders, who had always scorned his yearning to search for a prophecy. He was silent for a long time. Then he spoke. He did not speak the way he normally did. He also forsook the dignified demeanor of soothsayers and . . . sang. He pulled his veil down over his eyes, lifted his head up, and swayed like an ecstatic person in a trance. He chanted the prophecy in a melodious voice: "T'falam amadal, tekkam amadal, me tekkam? You depart from dirt and journey toward dirt; so what is the point of the trip?"

Stillness settled over the assembly. The group followed the message a long way and contemplated the metaphor for a long time. Then they cried with the air of someone who had forgotten something: "Did our master really say this?" The diviner did not reply.

Then the only man who bore antiquity on his shoulders intervened and seized the right to utter the decisive statement: "This is language that befits our master. This is really his idiom, and this is his wisdom. Don't you think it behooves us to obey?"

The proponents of migration argued their case by grumbling, moving their turbans closer to one another, touching their heads together, and pretending they were consulting each other, but Emmamma, who was older than any of them, allowed them no time. He took his polished stick and left the tent.

2

Tongues voiced objections, and mouths mentioned the Law's dictates that cautioned against any surrender to the temptation of the earth. Then the leader took charge of them all and, using the virgin's tongue, sent them a new message. This prophecy said, "Yassokal awadem yeway imannet meykka? What kind of trip is it when a man carries his soul along with him?"

The diviner chanted this with a noble, heartrending melody. Then tears leapt from his eyes. He chanted this for a long time before he sent for the herald. When the herald arrived, the diviner entrusted the mission to him. The herald went through the settlements spreading the good news of the prophecy. Then the virgin followed him to the diviner's dwelling, bearing a new prophecy. Via the virgin's tongue, the leader said, "Etekkam ettaqqlimd degh yohazan. Wherever all of you go, you will return by a nearby place." The diviner wept once more and sang the lyric mournfully while gazing at the distant horizon and swaying back and forth like people who are in a trance and robbed of their intellects by a song. He spent a long time on his private journey. When he finally returned, he dismissed the virgin and again sent for the herald.

3

He wandered in the wasteland for some days and returned from seclusion with an inspiration.

He summoned a man who was famous for his craftsmanship in constructing tombs and who was known in the tribe as the "Lover of the Realm of Stones." He sat with him outside the tent in the dusk of the evening. Sitting down, he asked, "Have you all finally realized that it is pointless to continue migrating?"

The Lover pulled his turban lower and began to examine the dirt with his fingers, searching for pebbles. He picked up a pebble in his right hand and deposited it in the palm of his left hand. He answered this question after a pause. "Whether we believe it or not, generations from now the Spirit World will make clear whether we were right or have committed a sin."

"Do I understand from this that my guest has preferred to join the doubting faction?"

"My master's guest does not prefer to join any faction. I'm simply talking about the will of the fates. The course of time will answer my master's question."

The diviner watched him inquisitively. He straightened his knee, raising it higher, and left his other thigh on the ground. He said, "I didn't, in any case, send for our dignified guest to debate the subject of migrations. I want to discuss another matter."

The Lover continued to dig in the dirt, collecting pebbles carefully in his palm. He replied, "I never doubted that, because the diviner would not send for a creature to debate with him a heavenly matter or a concern that we customarily reserve for the nobles in the Council of Sages."

"Not so fast! Slow down! I see my guest is about to lose his way. As a matter of fact, I did send for my distinguished guest for a subject that is intimately linked to the heavens."

The Lover stopped raking the dirt with his finger and looked at the diviner inquisitively for the first time. The diviner continued, "I thought I would surround my master's tomb with a building, and you know you're the only master builder in the whole tribe."

The pebbles tumbled from his left hand, and he picked them up with the deftness of a person who has lost a treasure. Then he replied, "I hope my master thinks well of me, but I don't understand the pressing need to build a tomb around the tomb."

"We have built a tomb to hide the bodies of the dead, and we will build a tomb to shelter the bodies of the living!"

"I really don't understand."

"Because we are a nomadic people, our forefathers taught us to erect a structure around the bones of a deceased man. We bury our dead today and travel the next day. But the Law has left us no statute regarding dead men we have decided to keep near us forever because they have become our destiny and our only path to the heavens."

From behind his veil he glanced stealthily at his companion, whose fingers he saw were working in the dirt with the ardor of armies of ants. He smiled and continued, "Today we guide our lives by the firebrand that comes from the tomb the way a nomad guides himself by the stars and the way our ancestors before us guided themselves by the light of the lost Law."

"I've begun to understand. My master wishes to replace the tent post we lost with a building that will play the role of two tent posts at one and the same time: the tent post that collapsed when the leader passed on and the tent post that will fall when we fold our tents forever to become food for larvae and grubs."

The diviner ignored the guest's allusion and spoke without any circumlocution. "People will gather at the tomb out of curiosity. Others will come seeking prophecies regarding secret matters monopolized by the Unseen and known only to the people of the Unseen. Nomads will also arrive, and tribes will send messengers to clarify signs or to plead for counsels. Communities will crowd together there, and the number of people will grow so great that eventually you won't find a place around the site to set a foot and the virgin won't be able to stretch out, lie down, or sleep. So be quick and ingenious about erecting a building. Divide it into three chambers. One will house the tomb, one will be suitable for the virgin's habitation, and the third will be a courtyard where sacrificial animals are slaughtered and visitors, messengers, and people seeking a prophecy are received."

A pebble escaped from his fingers, and he searched the earth carefully, digging in the dirt to look for it. Only after he had retrieved it did he ask, "What form does my master have in mind for the building?"

"To what form is my distinguished guest referring?"

"I meant to say that the form of the tomb has always been based on a circular body, because the ancients, when they built the first house for the first deceased, wanted to imitate the Spirit World. So they constructed the tomb of the wasteland as a replica of the eternal home. So what form will a structure built atop another building take?"

"The truth is that I haven't given any thought to this."

"My master knows that each body in the desert is destined to be circular."

"Actually this is the first time I've considered the matter."

"My master knows that gold is circular."

"Gold?"

"For this reason smiths work this metal into circular forms when they make jewelry and other decorative items."

"The truth is that I. . . ."

"The snake is also round."

"The snake?"

"My master knows that the snake always has some ulterior motive. If it is tubular and coils round itself, there is some secret behind that."

"What are you saying?"

"The desert also has a circular body."

"Hold on."

"It is said that the snake only coils into a circle to imitate the mother that gave birth to it."

"But. . . ."

"*Iyba*—the spirit, Master, is also in a round body."

"*Iyba?*"

"Since the *iyba*, or spirit, is round, we can deduce that the Spirit World is also a round body."

"Wait. . . ."

"For this reason, the forefathers insisted on making the first *edabni* round."[9]

"You can construct the building in any form you wish, but. . . ."

"I, Master, am a creature who has no wishes because I do not intend to disobey the laws of the Spirit World and don't want to prolong the building process unnecessarily."

"You're right. I meant to say that what matters to me is the building. The form of the building is the responsibility of the master builder."

"I thought the diviner would surpass me in enthusiasm for the Law of the Spirit World, especially when the matter pertains to the form of the rocks that will become a sanctuary for the people."

"The diviner is interested in every invisible matter, but what is visible and in public view becomes the property of the people."

The Lover of Stones stopped digging in the dirt and whispered as if to himself, "Wouldn't it interest the diviner to know that prophecy also has a round body?"

---

9. The tomb.

The diviner contemplated him curiously and asked, also in a whisper, "Prophecy?"

But the Lover stood up. He roamed far through the emptiness and transferred his handful of pebbles from his left palm to his right and then back to the left before he shot off without a word of farewell.

4

Before the Lover dispatched an army of vassals into the neighboring hillsides to start digging up rocks, he sent the Virgin a letter stating: "I will build you, by hand, a mausoleum unlike any your grandfathers built for their fathers and more splendid than any the desert has ever witnessed." It was said that the Virgin smiled enigmatically when she received the message but that this unusual flirtation did not elicit any overt reaction from her. She continued to respond with this mysterious smile whenever a girlfriend reminded her of the missive or whenever the Lover recited the message during their fleeting encounters in the open countryside, between the campsites, or during soirées celebrating the full moon.

The Lover roamed the crowns of the northern heights and harvested stones from the hills, using men who had time on their hands, the hoi polloi, and gangs of youths. When he had finished with nearby peaks, he advanced west, reaching the lower slopes of the farthest mountains. Then he stripped away their rocky surface and scaled their peaks till it was rumored that he was teaching the vassals and encouraging his assistants to imitate the expertise of the birds in making circular nests in order to succeed in chipping a round, beautiful stone. It was also said that he had tugged dolts repeatedly by their ears and led them to places where birds were accustomed to hide their nests—not to demonstrate the birds' skill in weaving their nests but to pluck from the nests speckled eggs that he thrust in the idiots' faces, saying, "Have you seen the marvels produced by birds? Don't you see that they do not merely build their nests in a circular pattern but also lay round eggs? Don't you see that a body that isn't born in a round house doesn't survive? Don't you know that a building that isn't round isn't fit for human habitation? Do you think I'm as crazy as you because I want to teach you to follow the path to which the desert leads us?"

These comments reached the diviner's ears. Local historians said that he never stopped smiling, perhaps because the Lover, when addressing the masses, hadn't used the same idiom he had employed when he spoke with the diviner that night. He felt well disposed toward the master builder, who did not slight wisdom by refusing to employ its language when addressing a people who are hostile to wisdom and who doubt the intentions of the people of wisdom.

The Lover finally began to construct the building. He chiseled down the boulders and evened out the solid slabs. In his hands rocks turned into lumps of dough. The people of the settlement gazed at him with admiration when they saw him busy shaping the stones with all the longing of a true lover. Their admiration turned to astonishment when they observed the three linked buildings rise with their noble domes. Over the tomb he built a circular house with a dome. Next to it he built the Virgin's house and connected the two by an arched doorway, which was also rounded. Thus entering the sanctuary meant transiting the Virgin's residence. Then he connected to these two houses a third dwelling that accessed the Virgin's house from the opposite side through an arched door with a round top set in curved walls. He told people that its name was "House of Sacrificial Victims and Offerings."

The building wasn't merely a marvel because the offspring of nomads customarily avoided buildings and in their travels saw only the graves of nomads and the tombs of the ancients, but also because the sages affirmed that not even in most of the oases had they ever seen anything that compared to this building in luxury and opulence. Not even the intellectuals discerned the veiled resemblance that the body of the building borrowed from the tombs of their forefathers and the graves of their ancestors. People attributed the building's form to the fascination of the Lover of Stones with the circular body and his strange belief in the circularity of every spiritual body.

5

When the Lover had finished his work, he sat down with the diviner, who praised the building and repeated, "Great job!" several times. He discussed the splendor of buildings he had seen in the desert's oases and concluded by saying the domes were truly captivating, although they were more severe than was necessary.

The Lover listened silently. Throughout the discussion he was bent over the ground, gathering pebbles and collecting them in a small pile. He spoke without turning his head, "Doesn't my master consider severity to be one of the attributes of the Spirit World?"

"You're right; you're absolutely right. But don't forget that we want the building to draw people to the tomb."

"People won't be drawn to the tomb by the fabric of the building if a love of prophecy doesn't attract them."

"You're right again, but not so fast. Are you casting doubt on the ability of a vessel to tempt us? Don't you see that nomads are merely grown-up children who must be lured with dolls if you want them to follow you?"

"I haven't invented any heresy, Master. Every game or sport has its ancient law."

"What do you mean?"

"I've said what must be said just as previously I did what needed to be done. I said that we have a duty to discover the symbol in everything. Similarly we must appeal for guidance to the dictates of the ancients when a difference about a matter arises between us. Or does my master belong to the group that only reads these dictates in the remnants of the Lost Book?"

"The truth is that I don't understand."

"The tombs of the first peoples are also a sign, Master. The graves of the forefathers are also a message. Everything in the desert is an ancient lesson and information that deserves our greatest attention. What I have done is merely to attempt to decipher the message. I have gone to great effort to decode the symbols of the dictates. The severity that has troubled my master is an indivisible part of the Law of the ancients."

The diviner did not respond. He drew a symbol on the ground. He dug in the dirt and pulled a stone from the cavity. The Lover continued, "My master should not forget that we didn't construct the building to honor just the leader; we decided to host the whole sky in it as well. If we want our hospitality to be complete, we must construct a house that imitates and resembles the heavens, because the house's circularity is borrowed from the circularity of the sky. That first day I told you that all exalted things are circular, because the Spirit World has a circular form."

"I find you speak of the circularity of the Spirit World with all the certainty of a person who has returned from a visit to the Spirit World."

"Each of us, Master, is a child of the Spirit World. Each of us has come from the realm of the Spirit World, and each of us will return there."

"I hope you won't think poorly of me, but the tribe's intellectuals have complained to me that your infatuation with circles is suspect and distasteful."

"I am sad to hear this from a tongue that usually is cleansed by the utterance of a prophecy."

"I told you that this is not something I have said; the intellectuals have said it."

"If it was the tongue of someone claiming a monopoly over the intellect who said this, then how remote these people are from the intellect and from mastery of the intellect! I don't know how a person can claim mastery of the intellect while denying the roundness of the heavens, the Spirit World, or prophecy. So may the Spirit World grant us protection from an intellect like this! Beseech the Spirit World to shield you from an intellect like this as well, Master."

He hopped. He hopped to his feet and disappeared into the gloom. The diviner called after him, "Not so fast! Not so fast!"

But he didn't turn. In the wink of an eye, the gloom swallowed him.

6

That evening the Lover didn't merely vanish from the environs of the diviner's tent but from the entire settlement. He vanished from the land of the tribe. No one saw him after that day in the northern wadis, in the encampments of the neighboring tribes, in the distant oases, or accompanying any of the caravans in transit. He disappeared because he had fled from the entire desert. He vanished, as if he had returned to his homeland, as if the Spirit World had swallowed him.

After his disappearance, reports circulated widely in the tribe when gossips gave free rein to their tongues, as is their wont during such periods. They said they had discovered the Lover's secret. They said that they had assumed he was merely a lover of stones when they called him "Lover" but that after he had fled they had discovered his passionate love for the Virgin. It was also said that he had told one of his construction assistants that he had kept his promise and built for his beloved with his own hands a mausoleum unlike any their cleverest forefathers had built in the desert. So what was the Lover to do in a land where he had buried his beloved with his own hands?

VII

THE DYADIC BIRD
OF THE SPIRIT WORLD

Music differs from all the other arts because it does not express Ideas or grades of the objectification of the will, but directly the will itself.

Arthur Schopenhauer, *The World as Will and Representation*, Chapter XXXIX, "On the Metaphysics of Music"

He was not forgotten and the anguish of his lyrics was also not forgotten, because he persisted in seeking to create what was lost in sorrows.

Søren Kierkegaard

1

The tribes knew another bird.

The tribes knew another bird in other times, and succeeding generations described it in praise poems that people still enjoy reciting today. Songs mentioned that he was a skillful singer and had only lost his marvelous body as a result of absorption in songs and fascination with melodies. But he was never absent from the world of the wasteland, because many blessed individuals saw him. Seeing him was a good omen for them, because they soon lost their bodies too and were liberated from captivity in the wasteland.

It was reported in histories that successive generations learned from experience that individuals whom the Spirit World favored saw its noble bird and soon shared its fate. They too lost their troublesome bodies and fled from the desert as the void became their homeland.

2

He arrived the way he always did, with the first breaths of autumn.

Yellow was garlanding the clumps of trees in Retem Valley, and the wind was variable. It blew from the East but then immediately changed and blew from the sea. Then it suddenly became so still that people in the encampments were sure it had departed to distant lands. Next it blew from the North at dusk with even greater force. Plants throughout the desert were agitated, the scant grass seeking the earth's protection swayed back and forth, and retem tufts and acacia crests responded with fervent trembling. The desert was singing with delight at the change of the seasons.

The bird came from the Unknown to sing his song as well.

He came to sing about the sad change in the trees' characteristics and to celebrate in songs of sorrow the mysterious, precious thing that autumn filches from the breasts of the wasteland's people every year. They feel really sad at its loss, even though they have never perceived its secret. They often feel sad, but would experience a greater suffering if they knew that this lost jewel is called "life"!

3

Narrators disagreed about his size, color, and behavior.

Some said he was a little smaller than the *mola-mola* bird. Others said he was much smaller than a *mola-mola*. A third faction swore he was the size of a worker bee.

People of the wasteland also disagreed about his color. Some said he was speckled. Others affirmed that he was silver with wings washed with chartreuse. They said this made him look captivating during the fleeting moments when he darted from tree to tree and light deluged his wings. A third faction went even further and said he had no color, because it was impossible to discern the color of a being no one had ever seen. They also claimed that the people bickering about the bird's size, color, or behavior were nothing but poets, who typically see what ordinary people don't, hear what other people don't, and say what others don't.

But such a claim did not prevent the tribes from arguing about the bird's behavior as well. Narrators said that he was terribly fond of valleys and preferred to hide in retem groves that autumn's yellow assailed, hiding for a time by the trunks of these shrubs before breathing through his pipes and beginning his amazing music-making. Others said he only descended into the lower valleys toward the end, because he sheltered in the crests of the acacias on the higher plains and stayed there for longer or shorter periods, slipping into the valley bottoms only at the appointed hour for singing.

Skeptics, however, attacked these narratives too. They said that the desert people still suffer from an ancient illness that antiquity itself named blindness! The proof is that they are still incapable of distinguishing between what is true and what is false, between what is good and what is evil, and between what is visible and what is hidden. If suffering this ailment had not been an everlasting curse for them, they would have been able to discover easily that the bird they describe isn't the same bird that fascinates them with his song. The bird they have always thought to be one bird actually visits the settlements in the company of another bird, his mate. Everything the tribes said about this songbird's size, color, or conduct does not apply to the bird of the Spirit World but to the bird's mate, which they typically view with the eyes of blindness.

4

The skeptics further discussed the bird and said that each body is divisible into two parts: the original and its shadow. They spoke for a long time about what is visible in the wasteland and what is hidden. They concluded that the shadow of a being is what the being's eye sees with its blind vision. The original of the being is what is hidden from the eye of blindness and perceived only with the eye of the Spirit World. The people of the desert are wretches who have brought incurable ailments to the desert. They are incapable of distinguishing between these two types of vision and are equally incapable of distinguishing between all the weighty contradictions.

It is said that this faction was the first to caution the tribes against the allure of the Spirit World's bird when they recounted the effect of his songs on people's souls and the domination of his tunes over the intellects of even the wisest intellectuals. People would all jump up and hurry to the valleys to hear his hymns of amazing sorrow. Noblemen, vassals, slaves, herdsmen, women, young men, and even the children would rush to the valleys. The bird would seize control of them with his voice, and they would stay in the wadis for days, frequently forgetting themselves there. They would stay as long as the bird did—not eating, drinking, speaking, or sleeping. Then they would become emaciated and quiver with feverish ecstatic trances. The jinn tribes that resided in their breasts—which they thought they had forever destroyed with the talismans of the ancients—would awake. The feuding tribes in their breasts would wake up and become ecstatic, foam at the mouth, and reel.

But the devastation affecting their chattels at such times surpassed the devastation affecting their bodies. Jackals were able to slay people's flocks in the pastures at will. Camels wandered off to other lands, where they fell into the hands of brigands and rustlers. Autumn winds blew and unruly storms plundered their tents, carrying away the furnishings. When people finally regained control of themselves, they discovered that the Spirit World had not returned them to the desert but had tossed them into the labyrinths of the wasteland for the first time. Then they were obliged to search for their way, starting afresh.

At this point the soothsayers intervened, thinking they should take charge of the matter themselves.

5

The soothsayers made the rounds of the tribes and dictated their call to the herald. They said the seductive bird wasn't one of the messengers from the Spirit World but a new device of the immortal enemy Wantahet. So people should be wary and extremely cautious. They said via the herald that the ancient, ignoble one had been unable to destroy them with bribes and it hurt him too much to take them with the weapon of seduction. Therefore he had devised the strategy of singing to annihilate their bodies, destroy their physiques, and devastate their homelands, because he had discovered their weakness for music. He had realized that nothing could annihilate creatures' bodies as effectively as singing. They also said that the immortal sorcerer was hiding in the bird's body this time just as he had previously hidden in the bodies of serpents. He had borrowed the bird's voice and slipped into the neighboring valleys to rob them of their bodies and souls through the domination of this voice, because the ignoble one knew their secret and perceived the weakness they had inherited from their ancestors regarding the voice and the delight of the voice. So he had decided to take them by means of the sovereignty of the voice. They needed to be on guard from that day forward against every voice!

Panic swept the tribes, and an argument erupted among the sages. Many attacked the edicts of the soothsayers. One faction tried to mount some opposition. Skeptics said that the diviners did not merely wish to shun the minds of the intellectuals, and never tired of repeating the lies they had fabricated long ago to lead the nations of the desert toward life (even though the tribes realized that they were merely terrifying claims), but today again they had come to drag the tribes far from the truth, claiming that they did this from a desire to prevent the community from going extinct, whereas they knew better than anyone else that they were preventing the community from enjoying the eternal longing for immortality, because they also knew that a being that doesn't become immortal unless he loses his body does not mind dispensing with the shadow body if through this sacrificial offering he can assume the body of light, the body of the Spirit World, the original body that doesn't know bodies.

In their opposition to the soothsayers, the skeptics went to the extreme of accusing their foes of depriving the wretched tribesmen of the sole pleasure the Spirit World had granted them and said that the diviners, by forbidding listening to and enjoying music, were not just imitating the severity of Wantahet but were appropriating his role and speaking with his tongue. In fact they were digging for the people of the wasteland that foul pit to which Wantahet had sworn to lead them one day. The soothsayers weren't soothsayers; they were Wantahet.

6

North winds frequently carried clouds to the desert, the valleys flowed with plentiful water, from the floors of the tents rang the painful screams of newborns frightened by the terror of childbirth, and the successive days destroyed many bodies, which then slumbered in the slopes of the mountains beneath piles of gray stones, but the bird of the Spirit World never stopped singing.

The bird never stopped singing, and his passionate fans never stopped descending to the valley in order to emigrate via song from this valley and all valleys—from the whole desert. Then they would see what they could only see through song and hear what they could only hear through song, and live another life that they could only live through song.

Their bodies grew emaciated, withered, and wasted away till they vanished. But they did not retreat. They did not want to return to the land of shadows, because anyone who travels far and explores other homelands beyond the wasteland will not return to the realm of the wasteland. He will not return to lands that can only be seen with the eye of blindness!

VIII

THE WESTERN HAMMADA

We know that while we are at home in the body we are away from the Lord, for we walk by faith, not by sight. We are of good courage, and we would rather be away from the body and at home with the Lord.

The Second Letter of Paul to the Corinthians, 5:6–8

1

During the second year, the drought became extreme, and desiccation, blazing heat, and blasts of the Qibli wind scorched the pathetic grasses left from the blessing of the wet years. Then the leader approached him.

The leader came to him and invited him to explore the effects of the downpours from transient clouds on the plains of the Western Hammada.

They set off on foot in the sunset dusk, leading their camels behind them and dislodging rocks along the way with their sandals. In earlier days, they typically had done this when the tribe was affected by some momentous matter that required private debate. Back then they would set off for the great outdoors, roaming on foot through the dark expanses of the wasteland like two shadows from the jinn tribes, striking their sandals against stones with childish stubbornness, exchanging a gesture at one time, allowing themselves to be guided by the circumlocutions of the ancients at others, adopting the language of the people of passion at times, and remaining silent for long, long periods. They stayed silent so long that the jinn who were spying on them concluded that they would never say anything. The Spirit World's spies decided that they would never reach an accord or assumed that these two men had secretly agreed to use a vile, unspoken language, a language that the clever strategists of the wretched human community appealed to in order to conceal their evil intentions against the scions of the people of the Spirit World. Dawn surprised them in the badlands, but they would not turn back till they discovered a talisman to protect the tribe against the evil of the affliction. So the most eminent jinn butted their heads against the walls of their caves in despair at ever detecting the secret and out of admiration for man's cunning.

This time too they walked along quietly. They walked in silence for a very great distance. They dislodged with their sandals a very great number of stones. They discovered the sign that rolling rocks with sandals conceals. They perceived the secret of the language that doesn't acknowledge the tongue, that rejects the eye's winks, that scorns the stupid signals of the finger, because it proceeds far into stillness, disappears in the whispering of the Qibli wind through the groves of the dry land, and bobs around in the open sea of the void with a feverish trance till the prophecy is stolen from the obscure rhythm. Above their turbans a moon swathed in a pale diaper began to spill a meager light over the wasteland.

In the faint light the naked land stretched away, covered with gray rocks that the limited light dappled with despair and gloom.

In the baffling stillness, the bodies of beings turned into ears and began to spy on beings whose bodies had also turned into ears. But the scattering stones wounded the diffident stillness and continued to gather the voices and to erect an edifice of language in the song.

They crossed barren plains, descended into valleys where the trunks of dead trees clung to their bottoms, and ascended heights that all vegetation had deserted, leaving on their summits monuments of solidity and boulders of rock that rose as high as haughty acacias.

Without employing his tongue, he said: "How harsh the drought is, Master! Is there a harsher affliction in the desert than a drought?"

He heard the leader reply, also without employing his tongue, "If it weren't for the chastisement of drought, the desert would no longer be a desert. In drought, too, the Spirit World hasn't forgotten to deposit a secret."

He fell silent. They traversed another expanse. Then in the same soundless language, he said, "But the desert is nobler without drought."

He detected the scorn in the leader's response when he heard him ask, "Do you want to deprecate the wisdom of contradictions and to devise for the homeland a law that the sky hasn't acknowledged?"

He was still again. They traversed valleys and plains. They clambered up copper-colored mountains. Then the barrenness was uniform and rushed away, extending forever. Over this harsh ground the pale light spilled down and proceeded to pursue the expanse until it turned into genuine gloom at the end of the horizon. As though distances had lost sovereignty over time and therefore could not interrupt the dialogue, the leader added, "It's not appropriate for a diviner to cast doubt on the blessings of contradiction, since he knows better than anyone else the qualities of an affair that fools consider an affliction!"

Smiling behind his veil, he said, "May I be excused, Master—doesn't the diviner have a right to forget he's a diviner and speak with the voice of the masses from time to time?"

He heard an answer as stern as a sword: "This is inappropriate."

He smiled again and replied earnestly: "I know we mustn't disdain the Law, even if the ignoble Wantahet was the first to give it to us."

He heard a suggestion of disapproval in the tone of the leader, who replied in the same language that shied clear of the tongue, "Did you say Wantahet?"

He responded at once, "Didn't the ancients pass down to us the claim that he was the first to say he did not do good because he knew that good would turn into evil and would not do evil because he knew for certain that the law of contradictions would transform it into good?"

The leader said, "When did it become right for people of the Unknown to propound the strategies of the ignoble one as part of an argument?"

He answered, "The diviner did not propound an argument. He repeated for his master's hearing what has been passed down from the first forefathers."

The leader said, "The diviner knows better than anyone else that the ignoble one prevaricates even when his tongue's utterance is correct. So, what about the intellect?"

He replied, "My error, Master, is that I wanted to be liberated briefly from this burden that you referred to as the intellect in order to enjoy peace of mind like the commoners in the tribe."

The leader retorted, "This is inappropriate." He rolled a stone away with an angry kick.

2

They traversed further distances.

Suddenly the leader asked, "Do you know why I wanted you to accompany me to the Western Hammada?"

He replied, "I'm good at deciphering the Unknown but have never been good at deciphering my master's intentions!"

The leader, however, ignored this jest and said with the sternness that has always been a hallmark of leadership, "You've always been beside me; I've never deferred to anyone the way I've deferred to you. You have been my buttress. You're the only person to whom I have revealed a secret, because you have never betrayed my trust. I have been isolated, and my solitude might have proved lethal but for your presence beside me. I have always doubted whether what is called a friend truly exists under heaven's dome. Had your conduct not told me that a friend must either be a companion or not, I would have been certain that a confidant was one of the many lies we devise and embrace to deceive ourselves. How can you not want me to choose you as a companion for a journey to the settlements of the Western Hammada since you have been my companion in the wasteland?"

The diviner replied gratefully, "I have tried to live up to my master's good opinion of me. I feel this is my obligation. If I have succeeded, may my master allow me to express my delight."

The leader inquired, "Are you delighted even though you know the terrors of a trip to the settlements of the Western Hammada?"

He replied, "My master's company is something that surpasses delight. My master's company is something greater than happiness. My master's company is a treasure in the diviner's breast that can only be compared to a prophecy."

The leader probed further, "Are you sure?"

He answered this question with a question: "Does my master doubt the truth of what I say?"

The leader, however, commented sorrowfully, "I'm not pressing this question because I doubt you but because I know how intensely tribe members hate to travel the route to the Western Hammada. I wouldn't want to compel you to do something you're not keen on."

He rolled a stone with his sandal and smiled twice behind his black veil. He said, "I didn't know that the route to the Western Hammada had a worse reputation in the hearts of members of the tribe than the venom of forest serpents. I also acknowledge to my master my negative feeling toward it, although I have a secret conviction that it isn't as evil as we think. In fact I've often thought that its evil isn't concealed in the terrors we attribute to it but that we dread it out of our ignorance of it. Since my master has chosen me to accompany him on this unaccustomed route, how can I decline his company, when it is an honor for which he has singled me out?"

The leader said, "I don't want you to do this for my sake, because the trip to the Western Hammada is the only trip that a man must undertake of his own free will in response to a call, not out of loyalty to a bosom friend."

He asked, "Does my master think that reading prophecies in the bones of sacrificial victims is an easier job than departing to our homeland in the Western Hammada?"

The leader answered, "I have never trivialized the dangers of prophecy."

He mentioned the terrors of prophecy in a sad tone that no physical tongue defiled: "Doesn't my master know that the diviner roams the desert and repeatedly crosses the Western Hammada before reaching the heavens of prophecy?"

The leader answered as sadly, "I have never doubted that."

Finally he observed, "My master can rest assured that the person he has chosen for a traveling companion is a man who knows the path and has returned from the settlements of the Western Hammada each time he has brought a prophecy."

The leader repeated solemnly, "I have never doubted that."

3

The moon didn't budge at all from its heavenly throne. The perceived distance had not changed once. The horizon had yet to give any glad tidings of the journey's end. The disc had continued to hang over their heads. The wasteland had continued to generate empty expanse after empty expanse, to spawn hills after hills, to sprout mountains after mountains, to cast forth plains after plains, and to split the earth with trenches, gorges, passes, valleys, and ravines. The two men met chasms face on as the distance swallowed terrifying crevasses, leaving gaping mouths behind them to become part of the opposite horizon. But the distance did not yield, and the dark ravines were interminable. These came from the north, flowing down from the crests of distant plateaus, plowing through the earth to create—with earlier torrents—a path to the southern lowlands before flowing into the waters of the great lake on the shores of which Waw had once stood.

After a silence that lasted an extremely long time, he complained, "How long the distances are! How enormous the desert is! When will the traveler ever reach his destination?"

The leader replied, "The destiny of the traveler is to submit to the route. The destiny of the nomad is to forget about distance. The sole antidote to distance is forgetfulness."

He asked with amazement, "Doesn't the wanderer dream of the blessing of arriving one day?"

The leader asked, "How does it benefit the nomad to dream of the blessings of an arrival when he delights in his travel? Won't travel in this case become the traveler's goal?"

He yielded to the leader's argument: "My master is right. I forgot that we are a nomadic nation. I forgot that we are a lineage whose destiny is nomadism, a lineage that does not care to celebrate arrival, because it knows that arrival is a shackle. We travel the path, because ever since antiquity we have made our living as nomads. The root of my fears, though, Master, is a dread of the labyrinth and isn't based on any desire to arrive."

The leader rolled away some stones that ricocheted off each other across the expanse, generating a syncopated rhythm. The leader asked, "Why should a nomad fear the labyrinth since he doesn't think of arriving as his goal? Doesn't travel in this case become a maze in a labyrinth?"

He replied, "I agree with my master, but my master also knows that the people of the desert fear no trial more than the labyrinth. Half of the talismans fastened to their chests were created to ward off the ordeal of the labyrinth."

The leader commented, "Desert people only seek what they fear. They passionately desire only what they hate. They only request protection from those they fear. Don't they attach sticks of *torha* wood to their dwellings to protect them from the evil of envious eyes,[10] even though they know it's a tree inhabited by tribes of jinn? Don't they consider the jinn their enemies? Then we see them rush to assist the jinn when wanting to learn news of relatives who have been long absent on trips."

He smiled beneath his black veil again and said, "You're right, Master. Nomads are always like this. Probably they have learned to sense the opposite in things because they have embraced the teachings of Wantahet, who taught them sorcery and extolled the capacity of desert lands to hide behind a borrowed veil."

The leader concurred: "I confess to you today that I am one of the greatest admirers of this ignoble one's arguments, even though I'm equally certain that the warnings of the Law against his wiles should not be taken lightly."

He smiled and asked mischievously, "Would my master have been able to state this view publicly while presiding over the Council of Sages?"

He glanced stealthily at his companion, but the leader was quick to reply, "Can a man state in public what he truly thinks after surrendering

10. *Calotropis procera* (Asclepiadaceae), also known as the Sodom apple.

his neck to other people and allowing himself to be shackled by sovereignty? You know better than anyone else how openly I struggled against the chains of leadership. But I finally yielded, not to humor the nobles—as dolts have assumed—but to obey the will of the fates that made me my predecessor's sole nephew on his sister's side. Today, now that the same fates have unshackled me and set me on a path that is beyond people's control and that the days do not alter, I will not hide from you my delight at my divestment. Oh, my longtime confidant, you don't realize that divestiture is a treasure; only one who has experienced it knows how sweet it is. Divestiture is the law of those who travel the route to the Western Hammada. So be patient till you try it. Then don't hesitate to bring me the news of your pleasure! Does my friend think I would choose him for my companion if I hadn't discovered that divestment is Waw, for which we have exhausted ourselves, searching all the desert's routes? I have always thought of leadership as a curse I did not choose and have always stated this view in public, because—from the heaven of divestment—I dare say that leadership is a million curses and that domination is an affliction that does not differ from any other plague. So today I acknowledge to you that I not only could not state in public then any opinion about anything—not just about Wantahet—but couldn't scratch my head in the council without upsetting the sages! So are you upset today that I sing the praises of divestiture?"

He was silent while they covered a short distance. Then, resuming the discussion, he seemed to reconsider his words: "We began by talking about the labyrinth. I don't know how we progressed in the conversation to divestiture!"

With the same zeal, the leader replied, "Doesn't the confidant see that the labyrinth is one of divestment's visages? Be careful, though, not to mix the labyrinth with divestiture in a single vessel, because heaven wanted to raise divestment several degrees above the labyrinth to prevent weak souls from aspiring to it."

He abandoned this discussion and spoke as if remembering something he had long forgotten: "But doesn't my master think it's time to bed down for the night?"

The leader answered casually, "Why should we bed down for the night when we don't feel tired? Didn't the forefathers teach us that the noblest trips are nocturnal?"

He responded in a tone that sounded skeptical: "Doesn't it seem to my master that this night trip doesn't care to end?"

The leader replied immediately, "This is the night reserved for people traveling on the route to the Western Hammada. If night didn't dominate this Hammada, why would the ancients have dubbed it 'The Sunset Hammada'? You should learn to forget excessively hot days and enjoy eternally moonlit nights."

They had not gone much farther along the path when other doubts flooded his breast. "I've wanted to draw my master's attention to a certain matter since the start of our trip, but it slipped my mind for some reason. I'm just discovering that we've traveled for a time without any food or water. Can a wanderer forgive himself for a mistake like this?"

The leader responded with a question, "Has my friend felt hungry or suffered from thirst? Does it hurt a wanderer to forget food and water if he is shielded from hunger and thirst? Don't you know that travelers on this road don't need to carry food or water?"

He did not mask his astonishment: "The truth is that I haven't felt hungry or thirsty. If there's anything under heaven's dome that can astonish me, Master, it is for a desert wanderer not to need food or water."

The leader kicked many stones and crushed a thick, dry plant before he replied, "The traveler on the Western Hammada road doesn't experience thirst because he doesn't experience suns or days. He isn't afflicted by hunger, because he has dispensed with the land of creation that belongs to the children of creation. Leave vanities to vain people and walk with me to the place where passing clouds have freely deposited their copious rain!"

Almost prayerfully, he asked, "Does my master mean to bring us a rainfall that we have despaired of receiving for generations?"

The leader replied with a promise that the tongue did not sully: "If certainty had not been my talisman with regard to the existence of copious rainfall, I wouldn't have dared choose my only confidant to accompany me!"

4

The barren land underwent a transformation.

The earth's mien grew softer, and the desert began to dispense with some of its grimness, gloom, and grayness. Then brilliant clay patches, which were covered with scattered, pale-colored gravel, were clearly visible, spreading in extensive, circular expanses culminating in low hills. But their crests were spread with rocks that differed from those of the Eastern Hammada. They were brighter in color, their size was smaller, and their appearance was gentler and softer. In many places the expanses of pebbles led to shallow valleys near the riverbeds. The leader told him that these are the earth's daughters, which gather the rains of the northern mountains to bring to the valleys of the Western Hammada. In these shallow ravines the two men found not only the plants' fleeting green but areas that had plentiful mires, other clay-rich lands where water was still pouring from them, and rocky riverbeds over which the heavenly spring glimmered in the moonlight. They discovered that water was still flowing.

The guide cried out, "We've finally reached the shores of the transient clouds!"

The leader added that the earth of the Western Hammada possessed qualities that the desert had not granted to any other land, because layers of dirt had accumulated atop the surface of the naked land and throughout the year it enjoyed a more temperate climate than those of the four corners of the desert. Its sky possessed an everlasting purity, and rains did not fall on it directly but arrived from the distant northern highlands via wadis, ravines, and trenches. The ravines and shallow trenches watered the nearby plains, and the washes carried the torrents to the lower deserts. This water was not merely generous with the earth but accumulated in caverns and caves while creating astonishing fens that ruminants visited throughout the summer months and that thirsty caravans, nomads, and wayfarers sought. What was left of this noble liquid after satisfying the needs of these deep caverns liberally provided for the depths of the great lake at the far end of the sandy desert, thanks to the lay of the intervening land. For this reason, desert dwellers said that the sandy Zellaf Desert was the desert most abundantly endowed with water and never tired of repeating a maxim that their tongues converted into a time-honored proverb whenever they affirmed that only the Spirit World knows what treasures the sandy desert hides.

The grass became more plentiful in the beds of the ravines, and in other tracts the vegetation grew increasingly dense and became real grass meadows. But the two men did not discover the riches of the expansive plains and deep valleys until they had traversed many mountain passes.

Deep in the valleys, retem shrubs were in bloom, the crests of the acacias were turning green, the jujube were ripening, and this thirsty tree was absorbing a generous draught of water as its thorns turned green and its tapered tips softened till they started to resemble the stings of scorpions. From the groves, startled *mola-mola* birds rose, and other birds sang prophecies in the tufts of the acacias while fledglings chirped in unison from clumps of grass.

The plains that lie between the gaps of the wadis were also teeming with plants. The fragrance of the flowers rose in the air and greeted the men in the valleys with a scent in which retem blossoms dominated. He drew the edges of his veil away from his nostrils to inhale the rich fragrance, which left him feeling tipsy. Tears came to his eyes, and he stumbled. So he quickly pulled the veil over his nose again. In the plains, which were carpeted with grass, it wasn't just flocks of birds that were circulating—herds of gazelles were grazing everywhere, racing across the grass. They plucked flower petals deliberately and lifted their heads, which were marked with white, to gaze into the distance while enjoying themselves and chewing. At the edge of the plain a wild goat leaned forward, bowed his two long, symmetrical horns, and began to scrape the earth with his hoof. He pawed away a tuft that rose some inches above the plain's surface and extended his striped muzzle to pull out a truffle. He gnawed off the top half and left the rest still in the belly of the earth. The guide called out, "I bet we'll find truffles too!"

But the scent of the truffles had found its way to his nose even before he heard the leader's call. He drew his veil away from his nostrils again. He wailed like a man possessed and then released a long, painful moan that resembled a dying gasp from an ailing chest afflicted with death's intoxication. He raced across the earth, dug out a truffle with his finger, raised it to his nose, and released another moan that was even longer than the first.

Birds hid their nests among *fasis* plants, bird's-foot trefoil, in order to conceal their fledglings from the hands of wanderers. From childhood experience he had learned that birds do not merely use this strategy to hide their nestlings but also to protect the nest itself. If a nest is discovered and the bird realizes that a hand has touched it, he will abandon it forever and fly far away to search for a location that no creature's hand can reach. In his childhood he had discovered that birds do not merely sacrifice empty nests but abandon their eggs as well if they find that human hands have touched them. A bird would stop singing and circle the nest for days during this mourning period. Then he would depart to another land where there is no trace of our filthy species.

5

In the vastness of these plains stood mounds of stones and many tombs of the forefathers. The leader provided good news that his tongue did not defile: "I promise we'll reach the homeland shortly."

He asked reverently, "Is the existence of these tombs of the ancients a sign we are nearing the homeland?"

The leader replied, "From now on you will walk through endless fields of tombs, because you know the Western Hammada is the first desert that the ancient ancestors settled when they arrived from the islands of the ocean, fleeing from flooding."

He admitted, "This is actually what we have heard from the jurists. But this is one of three narratives, Master, because the first one says that they entered the desert when they obeyed an order that banned them from their first homeland in the sky, the second affirms that they approached the desert after losing Waw, and the third says that they came from the islands of the sea after the ocean swallowed their cities, which were suspended between bridges. So which narrative should we believe, Master?"

The guide replied, "What matters here is the symbolism, not the stories. Notice that all the narratives concur in the existence of a first homeland for the first generations prior to all other homelands. They also agree on the existence of some heavenly anger or curse that drove them from their venerable homeland. Then they roamed the earth, and yearning for the motherland became a malady for which they have never discovered an antidote since that day."

They traversed another distance where the grass was more extensive, the trees were denser, and the flowers released their heartrending fragrance into the air. In the plains the gazelles bounded, and in the tracts lying between the plains and the wadis, lizards loitered. At the limits of the hills, herds of Barbary sheep accosted them.

He was amazed and observed, "I don't understand how the people of the Eastern Hammada can tolerate suffering from barrenness and perish from drought when near them lie gardens that would suffice to feed dozens of tribes."

The guide replied, "The first secret is hidden there. The nomad found himself traveling through the Eastern Hammada and relished that life, assuming that he was walking through the promised paradise. He persuaded himself, relying on habit, that he would definitely perish should he dare to leave for the West, because his foot had never trod the land of the Western Hammada and he had learned its characteristics only from the tales of travelers, the whispers of the Spirit World's inhabitants, and the mouths of lying messengers. So how can you rescue a community that refuses to attempt an exodus? How can people achieve salvation if they refuse to look farther than their noses? This reminds me of a slave I wished to honor. So I decided to manumit him. Do you know how he responded to this gift? He threw himself at my feet and kissed my sandal as he wept. He said that freedom is a burden that wasn't created for someone accustomed to servitude. He did not know what he would do with himself if he left my household. He finally said he would be forced to hang himself if I refused to change my mind."

He answered disapprovingly, "How horrible, Master! Now I have grasped why our tribe is marked for extinction."

The guide seconded this thought: "You're right. A tribe of this character deserves nothing but extinction!"

6

Bold streams flowed through the next valleys. Although the water had receded, the clay banks it left were still wet, and their feet sank into the quivering muck. They followed paths that were stones set in the slopes. Then they climbed terraces that soon spread out into plains that were carpeted with patches embellished by colorful flowers. In the open air, birds called back and forth with songs like young women's trills. Herds of gazelles trampled the body of the earth with their hooves as they bolted away, and the tombs of the ancient ancestors kept the two men company on swordlike heights and the crests of hills until these stopped them when they confronted the summit where the spring originated.

The guide said, "You should drink from the spring's waters if you wish to liberate yourself from the ancient load."

He asked in astonishment, "To what load is my master referring?"

The leader replied, "Didn't you tell me you long to free yourself from the bonds of the intellect?"

He responded, "I don't deny that this has frequently tempted me, but merely as a passing whisper, because we are a people who do not free ourselves of anything easily. We consider liberation from the intellect, Master, to be a harsh punishment."

The leader cried out, "Here you resemble the people of the Eastern Hammada and cling to the shackles of servitude!"

He began to tremble and protested, "We consider the intellect to be life-sustaining—possibly because we've never experienced life without an intellect."

The leader said, "Here you have won the key to the secret. All that remains is for you to take another step to open the door."

He was shaking more violently and pleaded, "But forgetfulness is grim, Master. Dementia is grimmer than extinction."

The leader approached him, leaned toward his ear, and asked, "Would it harm you to forget the people and terrors of the Eastern Hammada? Would it harm you to move from that barren land to live in a homeland that doesn't acknowledge space because it has liberated itself from time's rule?"

His body became feverish, and he began to tremble again, shaking violently. He complained loudly, "Dementia is an illness, Master. Forgetfulness is a terror worse than the plague, Master!"

The guide insisted stubbornly, "The lethal illness has a lethal antidote. You will never gain life unless you lose a fantasy you have always considered life. So beware!" The leader knelt at the spring, where water leapt from a fissure in the solid rock. Pure water like tears chased through the void in spiraling tongues that joined at times and separated at others, creating a mischievous bow in the air, before falling to the bottom, splashing on solid rock, scattering spray over the banks, and inundating the green, fertile soil that clung to the shores. The leader moved his veil away from his mouth and filled his hands with the deluge as tiny bubbles from the spray glistened and dripped from his hands like teardrops. He raised his palms to his mouth, which was covered by a thick mustache that had turned totally white. Below his mouth a dense beard was even whiter. A few small hairs grew upwards and were interwoven with his mustache, fully covering his lips. He swallowed. He swallowed with the slow deliberation of the noble elders and the ravenous thirst of the masses. Then his eyes were flooded with profound surrender, and the diviner saw in his pupils a gleam like tears of joy. There was a smile in his eyes. The diviner did not catch the smile on his lips, which were covered by the underbrush of snow-white hair. He did, however, capture the smile in his eyes, because the diviner was accustomed to seizing a prophecy from the sparks of a sign. He was searching for the secret of the sign when he found that a handful of the deluge was touching his lips too.

The diviner released a profound sigh before sipping some of the flood from his palms.

IX

FORGETFULNESS

Forgetfulness is a form of freedom.

Gibran Khalil Gibran, *Sand and Foam*

1

Gossips quickly spread the news.

The tribe awoke to hear that the diviner had succumbed to dementia's forgetfulness the previous day. They said he had thrown out his slave girl, whipped his slave, and ordered the herders to bring him his camels because he had decided to quit the tribe's encampment and migrate to settle in the Western Hammada. The ruckus grew more agitated by late morning. Boys raced from tent site to tent site, women emerged from their tents to watch, and herdsmen left their caravans of camels and retraced their steps to question servants about the news to satisfy their curiosity. Even the sages were compelled to gape as the bareheaded diviner chased teenage boys and the rabble while brandishing his tent pole threateningly. Others related that they had seen him respond to the call of nature between tent sites—still bareheaded—and then hurriedly enter the next tent instead of returning to his own home. The wretched slave girl claimed that he had thrown her out because she had refused to submit to his shameful desire when he groped her and wanted to sleep with her. She made a comment that soon made the rounds and was repeated by every tongue: "Iymmeskal. Ahadagh ar iymmeskal. Awagh wiggegh amghar wazzayagh. He's been switched. I swear he's been switched. This isn't the old man I know."

The ruckus continued.

The boys realized that the diviner actually had lost his mind and decided to have some fun. They provoked him with the tricks they typically played on madmen and the possessed. He chased them, cursing or waving his tent pole.

The sages consulted and sent each other letters via servants, herders, or teenage boys, but the hero acted before they could. He was the first to drive away the rabble and scatter them. Then he put his arms around the raging diviner and hugged him for a long time. Next he seized the tent pole from the diviner's grasp and carried him away like a bundle of clothes. He set him down in a corner of the tent, which had collapsed in the center after the tent pole was removed. Ahallum replaced the tent pole and ordered a passerby to bring him both the physician and the apothecary.

Before the physician or the apothecary arrived, the nobles approached the tent with the venerable Emmamma in the lead. They were followed at a distance by Imaswan Wandarran. They gathered on a hillock by the entrance. The venerable elder took a step toward the patient. He leaned forward to examine the ancient soothsayer, resting his veined, twiglike hands on the crook of his staff. His small eyes examined his comrade's face. The diviner's head was bare. His skull was crowned by a stern copper baldness, and meager little pepper-gray hairs, which were turning white, sprouted on his temples. White was prevalent and had also assailed the bottom of his beard, which was coated by grains of dust. On each side of his head grew a long ear; they were so long they hung down. These repellent ears resembled a young donkey's. As for the mouth's fissure, it was even more repulsive. It proceeded from the far side, setting out from the jaw's back border, plowing through the front of the face, dividing the heart's throne of beauty with an ugly creek resembling a woman's genitals, digging in the full moon's surface a crater that could never be filled, an abyss that was the reason that the first father, Mandam, was ousted from the homeland, because it swallowed the forbidden fruit. Since then it has not ceased devouring forbidden fruits. It has never eaten its fill since that day. Did the ancestors err when they viewed it as a defect and devised the veil to hide it from each other?

The odious cleft did not stop until it penetrated the jewel, disfiguring the entire face. It gathered by the other end of the jaw at the conclusion of its trajectory and so stamped the man with the brand of infamy. The grandfathers did not err when they considered the mouth to be a defect and covered it with the veil.

Emmamma said, "This isn't the diviner we know."

He stared in the soothsayer's face again and then turned to the nearest man to ask, "Can you recognize a man whose head isn't covered by a veil?"

Imaswan Wandarran dismissed the idea with a shake of his turban, and bowed his head toward the earth.

Addressing the hero Ahallum, Emmamma said, "I've never been good at speaking to a man whose face isn't covered by a veil."

Amasis commented, "How ugly the face is when a veil doesn't cover it!"

The venerable elder gestured to the hero, "Cover his face at once!"

The hero motioned to a slave standing near the tent, and the slave rushed forward as though he had been expecting this signal. He whispered something in his ear, and the slave leapt to a corner of the tent, returned with a black veil from a pile of clothes, and began to wrap it around the soothsayer's head while the elders sat in a circle inside. Ahallum, however, remained standing beside the diviner, following the winding of the black veil around the head of the poor soothsayer. The slave's fingers slipped between the folds of the linen as deftly as the wind, gradually circling the head vertically till cloth hung down on either side. Then he drew the coil in the other direction and held the other end right beside the diviner's mouth, fastening the fabric over the mouth with his forefinger and seizing the clump with his right hand to encircle the lower part of the face first. Then he lifted the tail up and wound it around the summit of the head twice to form the base of the turban. Next he slipped the fingers of his other hand between the folds to test the firmness of the bond without his first hand ever ceasing to pull the linen around the head. The fabric's tail, which had coiled at their feet like a serpent, diminished and moved to wrap the head with a proud turban that returned the former diviner to the council.

Ahallum sat the invalid down before the council and took a place beside him.

Emmamma asked, "Isn't it possible that the whole affair is simply a frenzied fit?"

Amasis replied, "The jinn possess a member of the tribe every day, but we've never had a crazed man strip off his veil, enter other people's homes, and struggle with boys outdoors."

Emmamma explained, "Possession may take many forms, and the acts of people of the Spirit World come in graduated levels."

Imaswan Wandarran interjected, "The desert has borne us on her back for generations, and our ancestors' bones have nourished her for generations, but we have never heard of a diviner being possessed by the jinn. Similarly we have never discovered in the lives of our forebears the story of a diviner whom the inhabitants of the Spirit World possessed."

Support for his claim was expressed in a communal murmur of approval.

Aggulli spoke for the first time, "You're right. The sagas relate that the jinn fear nothing more than soothsayers. We have also all heard in the sagas that soothsayers are a coterie that differs little from those of the Spirit World."

Amasis remarked despairingly, "We're used to relying on the diviner to decipher the talismans of the times. We've never considered what we would do when the diviner himself became a victim of the times."

Aggulli said, "This is a fault of the community not of the times. We should have learned that the times have never exempted anyone from their chastisement. The diviner too is a son of the community and of the age."

Emmamma leaned toward the diviner and examined his vacant eyes before asking, "Do you remember me?"

When the soothsayer did not reply, the venerable elder asked, "Have you forgotten your longtime companion?"

A faint glow shone in the eyes; then the council heard a voice, "Hee, hee, hee."

The nobles exchanged disapproving, astonished glances but clung to their silence.

The venerable elder said, "I am Emmamma. Have you forgotten me? Does a chum forget his crony so readily?"

"Hee, hee, hee."

The elders looked down at the ground and hid their sorrow in the figures their fingers dug in the dirt.

The physician arrived. Before he entered the tent, he ordered the servants to prepare a fire. He grasped the nobles' hands with rough palms split by atrocious cracks. He shook hands with them with both hands. Then he moved forward and knelt before the diviner. He took his hands in his palms and swayed back and forth a little as he said, "I wish I had never seen the day when the physician would be obliged to cauterize his master's head to restore him to the gardens of the intellect!"

The nobles bridled their grumbling, but it was audible all the same. Their fingers continued to trail across the earth, drawing pictures, tracing symbols, and building houses as if searching for the secret reason for this punishment and exploring the Unknown for an antidote for this unknown malady.

<h1 style="text-align:center">2</h1>

The physician cauterized the soothsayer's head with fire that day. The apothecary arrived and poured him a pot of herb-infused water. Then the invalid slept for several days in a row. Slaves kept watch over him by night, and the elders visited him mornings and evenings, but the patient evaded them and fled to the vacant lands to the west. Two days later, herdsmen returned him to the encampments. They said they had found him wandering barefoot and bareheaded, bleeding from the awful wounds caused by the physician's burns on his head and temples.

At dusk that evening a tall, thin, grim-looking man, who was totally enveloped in black, came to Emmamma's home. The venerable elder sat with him outside his tent and leaned forward, trying to make out the visitor's features in the evening's gloom. The man did not stand on ceremony, did not launch into the customary questions about health, plagues, and the news of droughts, raids, and the ruses of the times. He said instead that the diviner's illness was an ordeal that had caused him great sorrow and that burning the poor man's head had been a barbaric act that would not help, because the soothsayer's condition wasn't an instance of demonic possession. Next he surprised the old man by claiming he knew a secret that could cure the victim. People simply needed to allow him to closet himself with the invalid for a certain number of days.

The old man listened with interest. His fingers toyed with some pebbles, and he leaned so far forward his guest thought the old coot would tumble on his face. Finally he sat up straight and asked, "Will the reverend visitor be able to do for the diviner what the physician and the herbalist could not?"

"Medical doctors have never borrowed any science from the Spirit World, and the herbs of the wasteland cannot cure an illness from the Spirit World."

"Is the guest certain that the soothsayer's illness is a spiritual one?"

"A secret, Master, is a treasure you lose if you share it!"

"Is some sorcery at work here?"

"No illness would defy diagnosis if sorcery could not infiltrate our bodies."

"Are you a sorcerer?"

The guest smiled in the dark and did not reply.

The elderly man inquired, "Are you a rambler?"

The guest was silent for a long time. Finally he replied, "My master knows that we would never boast of a tie to the desert if we weren't ramblers."

The venerable elder wanted to ask about the man's tribe but realized that curiosity had pushed him over the line. He had violated the laws of etiquette and breached propriety by besieging the guest with questions that the Law forbade a host from tossing at the face of a guest who had not yet spent three days in his abode.

He whistled with despair. Then he ordered the servants to bring the visitor a vessel of milk.

3

It was said that the mysterious man expelled the servants from the tent and prevented visitors from entering the residence. He closeted himself with the invalid for a period that lasted a number of weeks. They also said in the tribe that they would never have received any news of the soothsayer and that the work of the strange man might have remained a secret forever if inquiring minds hadn't resorted to their ancient stratagems to satisfy their never-ending thirst for news of the elite. So they hired some mischievous boys, bribed them with dates, and sent them to spy on the activities of the man in black.

These boys said that they hid in a corner of the tent and saw the frightening man tie a palm-fiber rope to the feet of the poor diviner and fasten the other end to a peg driven into empty land opposite the tent's entrance. He left the sick man out in the open, bareheaded, and the lethal sun seared him with rays more vicious than the fires of the physician. So the first day the diviner sweated a lot and continued perspiring until his clothing was soaked. Then with their own ears they heard him beg for water!

The next two days the stranger left him out in the midday sun again. On the third day, with their own ears, they heard him plead with his tormentor to bring him a veil. But food was a different matter; they witnessed the atrocious torturer himself devour the food the tribe's women sent to the tent, leaving his victim hungry. These wretches swore that the man in black did not feed him a single morsel during the many subsequent days and that the diviner had not surrendered or asked his torturer to let him share the food. He sat nearby, directing his gaze gravely toward the void but returning occasionally from his despondent preoccupation to cast his jailer an enigmatic glance that gleamed with an even more enigmatic smile. He would toy with his veil and run his fingers through its thick folds. Then he would sway from side to side and the smile in his eyes would gleam even more clearly.

But the poor man broke after almost three weeks. The youngsters said that with their own ears they heard him ask for a crust of bread.

After this the man sent for the noble elders and informed them that he had restored the lost memory of the tribe's diviner and that they simply needed to supervise his nutrition if they wanted to restore him to his former state.

Emmamma was incredulous. He sat on his haunches before the frail body, raising his knees and thighs, and leaned forward till his turban touched the diviner's. He asked, "Do you know me? Swear by the goddess Tanit if you really recognize me."

The diviner lowered his eyes to hide the smile in them and said in a low voice like the whispers of lovers, "Do I need to swear by the lords of the Spirit World to recognize our revered master Emmamma?"

Emmamma clapped his hands and turned to the assembly of sages. He released a heroic shout louder than any that the tribe expected to come from the mouth of a venerable elder. He slapped his scrawny thighs, which resembled dry sticks, and repeated with childish glee, "Bravo! Bravo! Beat the drums of glad tidings, tell the maidens to fill the desert with their trilling, and slaughter . . . slaughter sacrificial beasts at once!"

He hugged the diviner and held him in his arms a long time. When he released him to allow the other elders to embrace their longtime comrade, everyone saw the tears in his eyes.

4

Emmamma said, "We missed you a lot."

Aggulli concurred, "Your absence seemed to last forever. We have grown accustomed to living with the absence of someone who has left us to travel far away; we haven't grown accustomed to enduring a yearning for a person whom we can see with our eyes but who doesn't hear our voice or answer our call."

Amasis exclaimed, "What a grim loss this was!"

The diviner responded, "I won't conceal from you that I missed you too. Had I not enjoyed the leader's company, my regret at losing you would have been even greater."

Everyone was still; the sages exchanged covert glances. Emmamma was the first to inquire in a voice that was somewhat disapproving, "Did you say 'the leader'?"

The diviner answered earnestly, "Yes. I traveled to the Western Hammada at the leader's invitation."

Everyone was apprehensive and quiet again. People hid their reaction by looking down at the earth. The venerable elder asked, "Did you mention traveling to the Western Hammada?"

"Yes, Master. The leader took me on a trip to the Western Hammada to search for rainfall from passing clouds. We found there a springtime that no eye has seen and that you all would never have imagined. I don't know why you cling to a life of drought in the Eastern Hammada and ignore springtime in the West, which you will never consider."

He fell silent and stared at the celestial void. Then he toured the horizons and rushed off through the eternal expanse. When he spoke again it was in a whisper, "I expressed my astonishment about this matter. Then our master told me that this is always the way with desert people. They enjoy an arid climate, because that's all they've ever known. They turned away from the orchards, because they have never gotten used to traveling West and have never known what the great expanse there conceals. I won't hide from you that I intend to return there once I have paid off my debts and discharged my worldly duties."

The venerable elder was the first to express his shock: "What are you saying? Have you returned to our domiciles or do I find you still traversing the encampments of forgetfulness? Don't you know that our scouts explored the Western Hammada inch by inch and returned two days ago, advising us that the earth there is scorching hot and that the rocks are almost molten and turning to ash on account of the fiery heat?"

He continued to roam through the remote distance, which was draped by the mirage. Then he observed in the same voice reminiscent of lovers whispering, "I don't know which hammada your scouts are describing, but I doubt that their feet ever trod the earth of the Western Hammada."

The elders stopped digging in the dirt and cast the diviner a pitying look.

X

THE CROW

Life pursues death,
and with death life begins.

Zhuang Zi

1

"Never in the desert will glad tidings from heaven be heard unless the tomb's stone drinks the crow's blood."

The sage asked the Tomb Maiden three times about remedies, and each time the Priestess replied with this same prophecy: "Never in the desert will glad tidings from heaven be heard unless the tomb's stone drinks the crow's blood."

The nobles did not know how to interpret this prophecy and gathered for many nights in the venerable elder's tent to debate it. They had asked the diviner's opinion shortly before he succumbed to dementia, but the diviner had not been able to offer any gloss for the revelation. The Temple Diviner herself was equally unable to decipher the symbolism of the prophecy, and the jurists did not discover any key to the puzzle. Then the Virgin's tongue repeated the statement with the same obstinacy and phrasing—as if this prophecy was a heavenly sign, as if this prophecy had been taken from some inalterable sacred tablet for which not even the number of its letters was arbitrary.

The first clause of the revelation did not confuse the tribe; it was the second half that provoked debate, caused disagreement, and confounded the most perspicacious people, the tribesmen who loved wisdom the most, and the ones most skilled at explaining dicta of the Spirit World.

The truth was that the second clause did not confound them in its entirety; the dispute centered on the meaning of the word "crow." Some said the word referred to the bird they knew. They declared that a real crow had to be sacrificed. Most people mocked that interpretation and said that the Spirit World always spoke in symbols. They were likewise unaccustomed to hearing in prophecies something that even the jinn could not accomplish—such as capturing a bird like the crow, which was proverbial in the tribe for its wariness, ability to blindside hunters, mystery, wisdom, and immortality. There was even a characterization of the crow in a riddle that stated: "Ed yohaz afus. Waritiggah afus! So near at hand, but never caught by the hand." This was because the crow kept moving between tent sites and never left the tribe's eyes for an hour; but despite its ubiquity, the generations that had tried to hunt it as a treatment for sorcery had despaired of ever bagging it—forcing them to search for relief from other creatures like the chameleon. They had left this aged immortal to later generations, who in turn discovered the secret for themselves. So their children ignored the crow, and the nomads forgot that it existed. What destiny could be searching for it today as a sacrificial offering? What enormous sin had they committed to prompt the dread Spirit World to impose this impossible condition on them?

This faction insisted on searching for the real truth in another place and invited the community to continue mulling over the matter, because celestial wisdom comes cloaked in mystery. But they had also learned that it could not resist a stubborn quest. Then it would be disclosed in the light of inspiration with all the suddenness of a spark shooting from a flint. If they wished to escape destruction from drought, they merely had to be obstinate, search down the corridor, use the intellect, and proceed down the path of debate. But the wait for rainfall became lengthy, and patience provided no consolation.

2

The first peoples said that when the Spirit World wishes to cleanse the desert of defilement by its creatures or to punish its people, it imposes on them either of two opposites: water or fire.

It either deluges the desert with rains—washing the land with floods until it drowns the creatures—or imposes suns that breathe fires on the plains for years, scorching pastures, destroying plants, and leaving there only trails of mirages and wraithlike fumes.

The first peoples also learned from experience that the heavens aren't stingy with water for the earth without reason, that the suns don't scorch the pastures in vain, that suffering descends on the desert for a reason that will not remain unknown forever, because the times, which address them with the language of signs at the outset, must necessarily reverse course one day and turn against the secret they concealed and expose it till finally every matter they were initially keen to conceal is revealed.

This time the sages exerted themselves to search for the scourge's secret too and discussed with each other a lot. Some found the cause in their subservience to the dirt and acceptance of the settled life that had always been their enemy. They had violated the law of nomadic migration once the leader's tomb became a peg that tied them to the earth. Others thought that the drought contained a broader significance and said that there was a sign in the matter, a sign like an embryo born without features, although the days would fashion a face for it. They had repeatedly learned from experience that secrets, even the most significant secrets, exist only to become known.

They simply had to be patient and wait for an act that would fulfill the Law's dictates.

The rabble were skeptical of the propaganda of the supporters of semiotics and spoke scornfully of their Law, which promoted a subservience that threatened the tribe's life and brought its people only destruction and extinction. These ruffians continued to scoff and express their skepticism even after the diviner succumbed to dementia. Then rumors circulated among the tent sites suggesting that evil had gripped the hamlet for a long time because the tribesmen had violated the statutes by trading camels, saddles, and containers of clarified butter to the merchants in the caravans in exchange for gold dust. They had taken these ill-omened flakes to the smiths, who had worked the ugly metal into vile jewelry for these wretches to present to their girlfriends as a down payment on passion and fidelity. It was said, too, that the diviner also procured the vile metal and had it worked into jewelry he presented to the Tomb Maiden, with whom many knew he had fallen in love long ago, even before the disappearance of Lover of Stones. In another version it was said that he had not disclosed his secret until long after the migration of the Physician of Stones and that then she had repulsed him severely. The Virgin was said to have told him that a virgin who married the leader and befriended prophecy would never stoop to love people of the shadow world. But the soothsayer did not give up. He decided to resort to gold because he had long known that this hateful metal can imprison the hearts of virgins and realized that Wantahet did not introduce it into the desert until he had tested its frightening ability to transform intellects, baffle hearts, and distort intentions.

Passion blinded the diviner and caused him to forget the Law's prohibitions. Then he acquired the forbidden dust from an itinerant merchant (according to another version: he acquired it from one of the tribesmen, who had secretly begun to deal in it) and had it cast as vile jewelry by a smith. Then he brought the present to his beloved in the temple. What is truly astonishing is that the narrators do not differ about the acceptance of the gift by the Priestess. Indeed they all agree that the Virgin took the jewelry and gazed at it for a long time before thrusting it between the stones of the tomb. Curiosity seekers swore that they themselves had seen her examine the jewelry with demonic, greedy eyes. She had held the gift up to the light before her face for a time and then had dangled the necklace around her neck and breast briefly while her lips smiled in a seductive way inappropriate for a beautiful woman who had chosen the Spirit World for her spouse.

The sages detested these reports. Many denounced passion and said that the curse was not actually in the forbidden metal but in passion, which shows no pity even to the people of the Unseen. The unwashed masses were amazed and said that the drought was a puny trial for a tribe whose diviner had acquired gold dust to present to a virgin who had dedicated herself to the rule of the Spirit World.

3

A thin, grim man, who was veiled and cloaked in black, paced outside the diviner's tent waiting for the dark to descend. He looked around him with the misgivings of someone who feared being caught red-handed. Then he penetrated the tent.

Inside he found the soothsayer leaning against the tent pole beside a dying fire and staring vacantly into a dark corner. He squatted near the hearth and tossed a handful of branches on the fire. Then he said, "I see that my master is still touring the land of forgetfulness."

The diviner did not actually return from his fugue and continued to stare rigidly into the void of the dark corner as if unaware of the visitor's presence.

But soon he returned to say, "How absurd it would be for someone who has explored the homeland of forgetfulness to settle for the lands of vanity or to savor lingering with people."

"I have never known a creature who lauded forgetfulness with your enthusiasm."

"How could a person who hasn't experienced forgetfulness or known its advantages praise it?"

"Why should we experiment with it when we know we will experience it one day for the first and last time?"

"If you all tasted the sweetness of forgetfulness, you would want to live it today, not tomorrow."

"May the Spirit World spare us this fate! We have children we need to care for till they grow up. We have livelihoods that we need to husband and develop. In the desert there are beautiful women and maidens we need to fondle and embrace on winter nights. So to whom should we leave all of this if we travel the road of forgetfulness before the appointed hour?"

"If you wish to escape from the manacles you just mentioned, then you shouldn't worry about them, because throngs of idiots will instantly assume your responsibilities."

"I fear, then, I would be the one deserving the epithet 'idiot.'"

"I have a superior claim to idiocy than you, because I want to bring outside a person who has grown accustomed to life in the dark recesses of a cave. I want to convince him that light is more beautiful than darkness."

"You're right. Leave me in my murky gloom and repay me your debt. Then go to the Western Hammada and live out your forgetfulness to your heart's desire."

The diviner abandoned his immobility and turned toward his guest to ask, "You?"

The visitor responded calmly, "Did my master think he was still advancing through his distant wasteland and chatting with the ghostly shades of tombs in the Western Hammada?"

The diviner sat up straight and tried to discern the features of the stranger by the light of the tongues of the fire that had begun to spread and blaze. He said, "I thought you were a man who once came to this tent to bring me back from the land of forgetfulness—thinking he was doing me a favor."

"The fact is, Master, that I didn't do you a favor that day out of any love of doing good, because you know no one does good these days out of a love of doing good. That day I did it because I feared my debts would go unpaid."

"What?" The soothsayer shouted this acerbic question twice.

His companion responded with a muffled laugh. He snickered for a long time before he asked, "Have you forgotten the debt or was the whole affair simply a strategy to escape paying? Was your supposed flight to the Western Hammada nothing but a flight to avoid repaying the debt?"

The diviner shouted in a threatening voice, "How dare you ridicule me? How dare you accuse me?"

"Hee, hee, hee. On my way to my master's house I was wondering why people avoid paying their debts and decided to ask my master why enmity insinuates itself between the debtor and the creditor despite the fact that the intellect says that debt ought to build sturdy bridges of affection between them. Did my master speak to me about wisdom?"

He leaned forward till the end of his veil almost landed in the fire. He released into the face of the diviner a hateful laugh like the hiss of a serpent. Then he leaned back and watched the diviner with a malicious expression.

The diviner said, "The Spirit World knows that I made a good faith effort to repay the debt I owe you. Had the heavens not intervened and the drought, which destroyed my herds, descended, I would have repaid the debt a long time ago. Don't think that a man can wash his hands of the burdens of the people of the wasteland merely by reaching the land of forgetfulness. In fact, liberation from the cares of the wasteland is the precondition for attaining forgetfulness. If I made the trip and was content to return after going half way, I only did that out of a desire to pay the debt. Had it not been for that desire, no antidote would have been able to bring me back to this earth."

"Hee, hee . . . but my antidote returned you to our encampments, Master. Admit, Master, that my antidote is more potent than the forces of the Spirit World. Do you know why, Master? Because it's an antidote that came to me from those encampments, because it is an antidote borrowed from the land of the Spirit World. Hee, hee, hee."

The diviner was silent. He was silent for a long time. Finally he said, "In the past few days the tribe's nobles have praised the one who returned me to them. I was thinking the reverse. I was telling myself that I would never forgive the specter who dragged me from the gardens of the Western Hammada to return me to the concerns of the world and the fetters of life in the tribe's encampments. Now that I learn this specter wasn't one of the shadows of the Spirit World, but a miserable man who merely wanted to retrieve a handful of gold dust, I see that I should punish him the way he has punished me. The only punishment I can think of is to refuse to repay the debt. This is your penalty!"

"What does my master mean to say?"

"Your punishment for your vile deed is not receiving your payment."

"Does my master wish to turn affection into hatred pursuant to the law of the creditor and the debtor?"

"Defaulting on a loan is a mild punishment when gauged against your hateful deed!"

"Why are good deeds in this wasteland destined to be rewarded with ingratitude?"

"Get out or I'll order you whipped!"

"You refuse to pay me and then order me whipped too?"

"Leave at once if you want to avoid falling into the hands of slaves with forearms stronger than iron chains!"

The guest leapt to his feet. Once outside he murmured a threat, as if uttering a prophecy to himself. "The desert has taught us to go and live in some earth other than the desert if we happen to acquire an enemy. Beware of living in the desert any longer, Crow of Misfortune!"

4

The tribe was destined to hear this prophecy again the day the diviner was slaughtered.

What happened was that the nobles' debate about the sacrificial victim finally ended with an agreement to slaughter a black, male kid, because the exegesis adopted by the majority affirmed that "crow" did not refer to the physical bird; the secret was hidden, instead, in its color. The special attribute of the crow was not its conduct, gait, or other less obvious characteristics but its blackness, which was its principal distinction. So they selected a black goat kid and brought it to the diviner to sacrifice on the stones of the tomb.

The nobles circled round the temple mount, and children and curiosity seekers patrolled the empty area near the tent sites. Then one of the vassals brought the bound kid and placed it at the soothsayer's feet. Busy reciting ancient talismans, he cast a vacant gaze at the naked sky. Then from his sleeve he brought out the bronze dagger and removed it from the scabbard. He bent over the sacrificial offering, and the goat bleated as loudly as it could. Then the diviner gestured to one of the vassals to come help him. The man put his knee on the goat's neck and clung to its throat with both hands. So the soothsayer drew the greedy blade across the neck vein, and blood spouted copiously from the throat.

It spattered and soiled the stones of the wall. The diviner withdrew his dagger and wiped the blood from it on the hair of the slaughtered goat. Then he sank the blade into the dirt near the blood offering's head.

Just then the specter approached the temple. He was awe-inspiring with his stern gait, broad shoulders, and black raiment. He passed by the nobles and proceeded till he neared the soothsayer's location. He said with the same strange rumble from which the diviner could make out the words only with difficulty that night: "I told you, Crow of Misfortune, to go and live anywhere but in the desert if you happened to acquire an enemy here."

He took the atrocious dagger, which was planted in the dirt, and stabbed the diviner in the throat. Everyone saw the lethal blade gleam in the light of the setting sun before disappearing up to its hilt in the priest's throat. The poor man emitted a weird rattle and seized the hilt with both hands. He leaned forward a little, and his eyes bulged out until onlookers thought they would drop from their sockets. Then he swayed as he struggled and fought to extract the ferocious blade from his throat. Blood flowed even more vigorously than the blood of the sacrificial offering, soiling his veil and flowing over all his clothing. When the gulled man moved in his attempts to save himself, his blood soiled the stones of the wall too. Everyone asserted that they heard the rumble of thunder far away at that moment, even though there was not a cloud in the sky. When they turned, they saw lightning split the horizon to the north, and they understood everything.

A voice cried out, "Did you hear what he said? He referred to our master as 'the Crow of Misfortune.' How could we have forgotten that all the tribes call diviners crows?"

At the moment the group snapped out of their stupor; some rushed to the diviner and others dashed after the specter, who had disappeared.

Ahallum pulled the dagger from the diviner's throat and the flow of the blood increased. The frail body shook with a feverish convulsion before becoming rigid forever.

Emmamma embraced him for a long time, mumbling like a mentally deranged man: "Here you have preceded us to the shore of forgetfulness, which you always wanted to reach first. And you, Master, accept your crow as a sacrificial offering!"

Thunder rumbled loudly, and the horizon blazed with lightning. People turned to see that legions of black clouds had begun to assault the desert from the North.

XI

THE DAGGER'S SECRET

Confucius said, "Fish were created for water;
man was created for the Dao."

Zhuang Zi

1

Thirst for the neck vein grows intense, desire for blood blazes, the tongue trembles with lust to plunge into flesh, the cutting edge gestures—craving to meet the beloved body—and the blade fidgets in the cavity of the scabbard, grieving for its loss and protesting against its suppression, cursing the punishment of confinement to these dark recesses. The body that is extended between the two leaves of the scabbard, however, remembers the talisman, recalls the symbols carved on both sides of the blade with a tongue of fire; so it appeals to the sign of the first peoples, who were the only ones to discern the dagger's secret. It propitiates the symbol by narrating the story of the beginning. So it talks about its amazing ability to pass through bodies, to swim in blood, to tear into the toughest meats, to glide between networks of veins, and to slip down ignoble paths to avoid chunks of bone. It whispers a secret, saying that discovery of articulated joints is the greatest trick in the whole trip. It gives to this discovery the name "trade secret." It concludes by saying that a nomad will not only double the length of his life if he discovers this secret but will accomplish his ancient dream of attaining happiness, because progress down the way of articulations is an amulet that protects one against evils and that saves a nomad from falling into captivity. *I open a door in the mute body, I make a path through the deluge of blood, I slip between the groves and disappear in the jungle, I scout for locations, I always choose the soft track, I avoid rough terrain, and I'm bent on fleeing from hard ground. The Way turns north. I go north. The generous Way curves west. I bend west. The path rises; I ascend. I glide up. The tour ends with an obstinate solid mass. I stop. I scout around. I turn north, investigate to the west, and retreat a step. I take two steps forward. I search the grim wall for its secret, for its hidden gap. I never tire of searching. I don't stop investigating until I discover the treasure, until I discover the cleft. I never struggle against the solid mass. I don't try to force my way through. Instead, flexibility, research, and patience will open a fissure for me in its body. I slip through the narrow gap like a serpent slipping through subterranean excavations. Then I shoot down a new Way without any strife, without any controversy, without any chaos.*

By using this small stratagem, I attain peace of mind and win my master's confidence.

2

I was born a slave like every other being in the desert. The secret of my existence is concealed in my blade, in my tongue. The secret of my master's existence is concealed in the handle. My destruction lies in my handle. My master's destruction is in the edge of my tongue. If he seizes the hilt, he obtains life. If he releases the hilt, others seize it. Then the blade becomes his fate. The blade can bring destruction, because destruction entered the desert inside my tongue. That was why the first peoples created the forbidding scabbard to hide my intentions, to restrain my desire, and to suppress my eternal craving for a brother's throat.

In the short distance lying between the hilt and the beginning of the blade stretches the law of life and the law of death. A person came who succumbed to temptation and yielded to desire; so he took possession of the hilt. The desert bowed down to him because he possessed the hilt. Then he became sultan over the desert. The blade became the fate of anyone who hesitated. These people became slaves, captives, and mamluks in the sultan's kingdom.

No one in the desert knows how the sultan was able to discover the secret of the hilt and the secret of the tongue. Most probably the jinn tribes whispered the matter to him, because the desert people realize that members of this mysterious tribe become allies of the sovereign once he grasps the terrifying hilt. By night they tell him what he should do during the day. They brief him on the intentions of evildoers even before these miscreants tell themselves what they intend to do. It has been said that the sultan's desire to possess the hilt originated with the jinn. So he would not go to sleep without first wrapping his fist around the hilt. Later, he fastened his fingers to the hilt with a rope of palm fiber. Later still, he secured his fingers around the hilt with straps of fresh leather, and once these straps dried, his fist and the hilt formed a single hand. It has been said that this ruler surpassed in cleverness even the jinn sages themselves. So their demons feared him, and their clever schemers were afraid of him. Then it came to pass that he subdued them and they became his servants; he put them in charge of his enemies among the people of the wasteland. His sovereignty over the desert was unchallenged because aspirants to power despaired of ever seizing hold of the hilt now that it formed a single body with his hand.

3

The jinn were the first to discover the horror of metal. Then they avoided blades and fled from the tongue to the farthest kingdoms. It was said in one report that they experimented with it. It was said in another report that they weren't stupid enough to try it themselves but observed its domination over the people of the wasteland when the sultan of the wasteland mastered them with a hand strapped to the hilt. So they read this as a prophecy.

No one knows how their situation was disclosed and how people learned their fear of blades, but the people of the desert soon started using blades to take vengeance on the residents of the Spirit World. They stripped the tongues of their scabbards and affixed lethal blades near the heads of infants, whom the jinn customarily kidnap in their swaddling clothes to swap for children from their own community. Then they terrified the wretches and expelled them to the farthest corners of the badlands.

From that day forward, the body of the dagger has been an amulet. But fools neglected the hilt and left it hanging in the air. Then enemies took possession of it and aimed it at the chests of their children one day.

4

Today, as well, the dagger seeks help from the talisman sketched on the tongue; the ancient talisman finds a way for it to escape from the flask. It dives into the void of the sky, bathes its ravenous tongue in the flood of light, and plucks, from a dusk-time rendezvous, a prophecy that will eventually carve out an existence for it with the edge of the blade.

The dagger emerged from its prison, and the blade rattled in the throat while it licked the blood of the black kid. It rattled with a sarcasm that wasn't grasped because it wasn't understood.

The hilt disappeared in the master's palm, and the blade plunged into the flesh of the neck. It followed its ancient Way, cut the network, severed the ropes of arteries, and penetrated the veins in which the fountain of life flows. It mangled the rough pass, severed the strings, crossed into the stream to drink from the copious deluge. But it would be absurd for the tongue of prophecy to quench its thirst from the spring of the lie.

5

The tongue leapt from the cavity, and the blade fled from the body of the sacrificial offering. It descended nearby and hid its thirsty head in the dirt. The master released the hilt; then the long fettered demon of the blade liberated itself. It circled the heavens in an instant, and when it returned to the confines of the wasteland with a prophecy, the messenger of the Spirit World had ascended the temple mount. He approached the temple stealthily—thin and stern. Bending down, he seized the hilt at once, exploiting the master's error. So he preceded him to the lethal throne, since the master needed to receive his punishment at once, because the sovereign forgot that the hilt would revert to being a blade if the commander set it aside for even an hour.

The blade settled in the throat of the master of the blade that evening, because the Spirit World wanted to exchange prophecy for the lie and wished to tell the diviner that the person possessing the hilt of the dagger should be extraordinarily cautious, because the sovereign who errs once inevitably errs for the first and last time.

XII

THE TORRENTS

Water, gentle, yielding, and pure, is good for washing away the filth of men. Therein lies its humaneness. When one looks at it, it may appear black or it may appear white. Therein lies its subtlety. When measuring it, one cannot use a leveling stick as with grain, but when the vessel is full, it stops accumulating. Therein lies its rectitude. There is no place into which it will not flow, yet it stops on reaching its proper level. Therein lies its righteousness. Men all rush upward; it alone rushes downward. Therein lies its sense of humility.

The Guanzi, "Water and Earth"

1

The north breathed winds that diffused the fragrance of moisture; the gloomy horizon encircled the northern mountains with a noble belt that always took on the color of dawn; the distant clouds grew thicker, presaging an assault; bolts of lightning ripped through their august gloom with an insistent gleam that twisted in tongues as fast as fiery whips only to die out with a swiftness reminiscent of the mystery of prophecy.

The wait did not last long.

The black clouds assaulted the thirsty wasteland like enemy hordes. The storm advanced as if wishing to caress the naked badlands and threw down at first large drops the size of the foam that fine camel stallions expectorate in mating season. Then the rain poured down. It poured down plentifully. The downfall stirred up dust in the void and the thirsty earth was taken by surprise. It spluttered with the insatiable appetite of someone who always wants more and then, overcome by greed, chokes on his serving and spits back up what he has swallowed. The expanses paved with stone slabs drank first; then the deserts covered with carpets of pebbles imitated them. Next the deluge flooded the terraces and slipped secretly down natural conduits to the ravines, which carried it to washes coated with layers of soft earth. Then the sandy valley bottoms seized the water with the longing of passionate lovers. Meanwhile the clay lowlands drank in less time and the water rose again to collect in level patches, but this stasis did not last long. The ravines pushed down a new heavenly stream, and the earth received from the sky a new supplement. The upper valleys brought a greater share. Then the demon in the flask of the patch of ground grew restless and rushed off on a course that began with a humane, rational chain but that increased in insanity as it advanced. This insanity was fed by the many ravines that intersected the valley's banks, and the flood borrowed nourishing momentum from the sky. As these gifts accumulated, the frenzy increased. The water abandoned its own name to become a demon that had appropriated the name torrent!

2

The torrent outstripped the cloud's slow advance and reached the farthest deserts downstream, surprising creatures that roamed the wasteland over which shone the harsh rays of a cloud-free sun.

The demon grew increasingly delirious and stretched out a stealthy hand to seize sacrificial offerings. It snatched bird nests from the trunks of the retem shrubs. Small eggs marked with murky, dark colors floated to the surface, and newborn chicks covered in yellow down appeared at the tip of the voracious tongue, fussing and releasing cries of farewell. Meanwhile the mothers fluttered over the insane current with the alarm of a tribe subjected unexpectedly to a raid.

In areas further downstream, in the expanses where the earth of the valley bottoms was soft and the burrows many, the demon's hand reached down to extract victims from the deepest holes. Mice fled from aggressive snakes, snakes fled from brutal hedgehogs, and hedgehogs fled from terrifying men. The demon put its sacrificial victims in its satchel and stormed through other clefts to take other victims from other species: hares, dung beetles, lizards large and small, and young gazelles. It did not acquire more significant victims until it reached the wide lower valleys, where herds of sheep and camels grazed and herdsmen chatted around bonfires, entertaining themselves by exchanging riddles, vying in poetry, and raising their voices in mournful songs. Then they returned from the realms of longing to discuss again the punishing drought and the vacillating flow of time. The demon surprised the lower pastures to seize the most significant sacrificial offerings.

It surprised the herdsmen by night. Then it caught the sheep, goats, and kids off guard and claimed a terrifying share of the herds. Next it attacked the owners of the herds, corralling them on small islands that rose in the hearts of the large, flooded lower valleys. At first it carefully laid siege to its victims while waiting for the support it would receive from the deluge via other tributary ravines, water courses, and wadis. It grew stronger with the abundant rain in the North when the earth became saturated with water and propelled a plentiful amount to the lower valleys. The deluge poured forth, the water level rose in the valley bottoms, and frightening waves gushed on to the farthest plains. The current swept away the meager islands, and the demon washed over its stranded victims to throw them into the dreadful floodwaters. The herdsmen fought back courageously. They clung to retem trees and deployed palm-fiber ropes, contending with the rising waters with poles, but the demon also fought desperately and did not yield until it had seized human victims.

The torrent dragged its victims to the lowlands in the Southern desert. There sand swords—longitudinal dunes—obstructed it. So it slowed, became calmer, and its tongue plunged underground to bury in the abyss the victims it had carried from the Northern deserts.

3

On the heights, on the open plateau of the Hammada, the tribe abandoned their tents, which were threatened with flooding, and fled to the hills, to high places, and to the mountain slopes. In these locations, groups of children, women, and old men gathered. They wrapped themselves in whatever covers they had been able to carry, and the clever strategists among them pulled from their clothes treasured sticks of firewood they had brought wrapped in scraps of linen to keep them from getting wet. They stretched themselves over their wood to protect it from the rain with their bodies. As the children's crying grew louder and adults started complaining they were cold and hungry, the cunning planners gathered in circles, shielding their heads and bodies with cloths, and began to struggle with their flints to beg for fire. They struggled for a long time before sparks shot out. Then they struggled for an even longer period before these sparks ignited the linen wicks and the smell of smoke rose from the scraps of fabric. They struggled further before successfully setting the wood on fire as a tongue of flame rose from it. Then they began to blow on the nascent tongues of flame to encourage the fire to crave the sticks, which none of their precautions had kept from growing damp.

The herdsmen in the lower valleys, for their part, hastened to move their herds from the deep valley bottoms during the rain's first assault and sought refuge on the heights overlooking the valleys. They grieved over their lost livestock and helped each other rescue victims stranded by the torrents on islands in the wadis. They threw them ropes or tossed them poles to use in fending off the current when the flood waters spread and the rising water level threatened them. When evening fell, the herdsmen discovered that the lethal demon had separated their company and scattered them over the heights, hills, and banks. They called loudly to one another, asking in the first hours of the night about losses. Then they were still for a long time. The sound of the surging water rose; the water dominated the conversation instead of them for a long time. But the words of the torrent frightened them and roused the ghoul of loneliness in their souls. So they raised their voices in song and sang all night long.

In the wadi bottoms, the torrent sang.

On the cliff tops, the shepherds sang.

4

The clouds' assault lasted a day, two, or three before the Unknown drew a sign across the horizon; a rainbow appeared to indicate that the storm clouds had withdrawn.

In the sky the sun's disc, deprived of its fiery rays, shone myopically through bands of cloud and fog—like a full moon over the desert. Even after these diaphanous clouds dissipated and the fogs lifted, the celestial goddess cast a tolerant eye at the wasteland's creatures—as if she had finally decided to relax her former oppression. The humidity, however, evaporated once the clouds had scattered. Then the barren lands paved with slabs of stone dried out, followed by the terraces carpeted with pebbles and small gravel. The moisture burned off the body of the clay lands and then the sandy tracts till no trace of the rain lingered in the upper desert except for low-lying washes soaked by the deluge. All the same, the torrent continued to rave, jabber, and prattle in the valley bottoms.

The scattered remnants of the tribe returned from their sojourn in the heights. They moved through their retreats, set out foundations, raised the tent poles, searched for lost possessions and missing items that they typically forfeited whenever a blessing arrived and when the Unknown granted them rains.

They were so preoccupied by searching for necessities, possessions, and chattels that they forgot about themselves and ignored the birth of birds in the skies, which were still obscured by fogs. The children would go out to play in the mud puddles in the neighboring plains. So they were the first to discover the appearance of sprouts growing from cracks in the rocks and raced home with the good news.

XIII

THE SACRIFICE

*Just as children gather round their mother,
things in this world thirst for ritual sacrifice.*

Rig Veda

1

"Water in the sky, and water on the earth: if you lack water in the sky, search for water in the earth." The tomb's Diviner uttered this prophecy aloud, inscribed it on a piece of leather with a metal skewer, which she had heated in the fire, and then sent it to the Council of Sages. These nobles, however, were so used to cryptic expressions in news from the Spirit World that they could not believe they had been granted a prophecy that did not require extensive exegesis. So they searched for the hidden meaning beneath the apparent one for nights. They were skeptical of the apparent meaning, saying that the Law had cautioned them against accepting statements at face value, because anyone who trusted what he saw, believed what he heard, and accepted what he was given met a fate like the traveler who violated the law of the road by leaning over a rope left in the middle of the trail. After he took it and placed it around his waist, the rope changed into a snake that killed him during the night when he lay down to sleep.

The elders' debate lasted for days. Finally they sent a messenger to the Temple Priestess with a question that would put an end to their doubts. They received in return a square of leather with the prophecy two days later: "Water in the sky, and water on the earth: if you lack water in the sky, search for water in the earth."

They abandoned their debate and consulted with each other. They scouted all four directions and reached a consensus in favor of the depression that lay south of the plain. Then they sacrificed a young billy goat and began to dig.

2

The poets sing in praise of the Red Hammada's beauty, calling it the sky's true love. It rises far above the elevation of the other deserts, reaches into space, and pursues distant stars on its way to unite with its beloved. It utilizes shanks of solid rock and strives to reach the heights on pillars of mountain peaks. But it stops halfway for a reason the ancestors did not explain, not even in the traditions of the first fathers. The later generations did inherit from their grandfathers sad songs that compare this patch of ground suspended in the celestial void to a nomad who chose solitude, not because he wanted to flee from people but because he pitied people. Then he lost his way, and the labyrinth became his sole homeland. The Hammada that swims in space's expanses is another vagabond homeland. Thus it has not obtained its share of water from the sky, thirst has parched its lands, and it is incapable of chasing after the waters that flee to lowlands of the Southern desert (where the lake of Great Waw once swelled and where a mighty sea of sand cowers today) or slip to the North to pour their gift into the distant sea. So it is said that the Red Hammada is the only desert area that feeds neighboring regions with its blood, gives other deserts the secret of life, and chooses drought as its destiny—pursuant to the Law's dictates, which say that a parched land is nobler than wet ones.

Despite the terrifying elevation, despite the deluge's flow to the North and South, the suspended desert found a way to conceal its waters in severe, solid stone. Thus since the most ancient times the nomad's hand has reached down to dig in solid boulders shafts so deep that the eye cannot discern the bottom. Later desert dwellers called these passages "wells."

From the West appeared unidentified ancestors, who settled there. They enjoyed living in the expanses of the suspended body. They were, however, soon caught off guard by the heat and tasted the bitterness of thirst. So they split open the earth's belly and crumbled the solid stone with their hands. They were not destined to reach water for several generations. For years tribes have passed down to the next generation the well of the Western Hammada, giving it many names, which changed from one generation to the next. The last of these was Efartas.

People came from the South and met the same fate as the ancient people from the West. They dug into the dirt with a zeal that surpassed the ardor of rats. Far down they reached water and gave the Southern well many names. The last of these was "Thirsty Man's Well."

Peoples arrived from the North and proceeded to search for their share of water in the depressions of the awe-inspiring mountain ranges that characterize the North. Local historians relate that the luck of these peoples was worse than that of the other tribes. They dug very many wells before they drew water from two called Awal and Emgharghar. Herdsmen still discover the vestiges of all these wells and find their mouths sealed with circular slabs of cut stone. They are delighted, exult, and call back and forth to each other, thinking that they have discovered a new mouth for the earth. But their joy turns to sorrow when they discover that the well is nothing but an empty pit. Despite their disappointment, the sages did not despair. Frequently they found random wells that were more like cisterns, because their water was not merely fetid, bitter, or weird smelling but the quantity was limited and was exhausted as soon as herds of camels visited it once or twice.

The strangest, deepest, and oldest well, however, is Harakat, which is situated at the heart of this suspended planet. In their songs poets refer to it as "the gift from the people of passion" or "the lovers' miracle," because narrators say that a lover who was a member of the first tribes dug it as a symbol of fidelity to his beloved, who was coming from the East to marry him when thirst killed her en route. The lover wept a long time for her. Then he realized that his glory would come not from weeping for his beloved in verse but in conquering the ghoul that had taken her from him.

The lover searched the Hammada from the extreme East right through the central areas inch by inch and scoured it with an army of hired assistants, servants, and vassals. Then he did not discover even moisture left behind by floodwaters in the lowest strata of the earth. All the same, he hired more workers, purchased armies of slaves, made use of people coming from every direction, and proceeded to fight the rock and to chisel away the solid stone without succeeding in discovering the treasure. The tops of many wells caved in during this struggle as the earth claimed its sacrificial offerings repeatedly through cave-ins. Many slaves fled and even more hired hands quit, but the lover bought more slaves to replace those who had fled and paid the new workers even more liberally, replacing the army of explorers who had quit. So the excavations continued with even greater zeal each time he welcomed a new army into his ranks as recruits. Other tracts of land were harrowed as time passed. The commander of this army was the only person who wasn't conscious of the passage of time, who did not notice the changing seasons, and who did not hear the screams of the many babies who were born. Likewise information about people who grew tired and lay down beside their fathers beneath piles of rocks in the tombs of the slopes escaped him. He kept stooping over the earth, inspecting its markings as if reading in them a prophecy that confirmed that life did not consist of trekking like nomads across vast expanses in search of a rendezvous beyond the horizon. Instead, life meant kneeling on the ground and searching for treasure in the deepest pits. For this reason, wrinkles formed on the lover's skin, and networks of veins showed on his face and arms. His heart, however, did not grow old, and the sparks in his breast did not die out. In this way he lost all his peers and contemporaries, all the members of his generation. He became his generation's sole heir.

He was his generation's heir because he did not follow his generation's path. His peers disappeared because they spread over the earth, seeking something that did not exist. He differed from his peers because he did not move across the earth and did not waste time on what the earth lacked. His contemporaries had long ago passed away, bequeathing life to a person who had renounced life and did not wish to inherit what other people considered life. The lover had forgotten the goal of the desperate digging and had forgotten the reason for this lethal struggle, because he had forgotten himself for an even longer period. So he did not even lift his eyes from the earth when his workers came to him and brought him the good news that the solid rock had finally been vanquished and that water was spurting from the hard stone.

3

Songs celebrate the water that gushed from the granite with all the abundance of a spring and continued to flow into the wasteland during all the bygone years after the lover's age. In subsequent generations, however, the treasure began to retreat, and the earth started to swallow its water, which disappeared from sight. Reaching the water required a sturdy set of palm-fiber ropes. Soon tribes were talking about travelers who headed to the well but perished while circling the mouth and looking down the pit at the sight of the water, because they hadn't provided themselves with sufficient quantities of rope. In other times, clever planners attempted to remedy the problem by leaving piles of palm-fiber ropes at the well's mouth as a benefaction for wayfarers. But sun and dirt got to the ropes before travelers did and destroyed them in short order. Then the sages introduced a new law that in time became a noble tradition. It required everyone who came to the well—whether herdsmen, caravan owners, or nomadic tribes—to bring a quantity of rope to leave behind at the mouth of the well in exchange for water. So piles of rope accumulated by the mouth of the well, and bulky clusters of rope littered the area in networks that stretched here and there. Coils of palm-fiber ropes transformed the adjacent bare land into a veritable rope jungle. The savage sun devoured some ropes as the fiber turned white; dust and grit mangled the rest. Not only did the color fade, but the rope became frayed and disintegrated. Other piles more recently created looked brand new from a distance. A person seeing them imagined that he would inhale their fresh scent when he approached—the scent of fresh, moist palm fiber, the smell of the oases, and the aroma of dates and of seasons of ripe dates at the beginning of fall.

Nearby, in increasing numbers, other ropes woven from goat or camel hair piled up. These ropes were braided with greater expertise. Poets report that they were woven by the fingers of beautiful women who trembled for fear of getting a bad reputation or of being disgraced. So they took extraordinary care and wove the ropes with the same apprehension they felt when weaving nose ropes for *mehri* camels or the saddle ropes for gallant riders, because they were certain that the strangers who frequented the well's mouth would inquire, ask each other, and figure out some stratagem to determine who had made the rope. If she had done a good job, they would write poems praising her; otherwise they would attack her with satirical songs.

Pride of place in the epics of the ancient generations, however, was allotted to the amazing ring around the mouth of the well. This polished disc, which was no more than a single cubit across, was sternly rounded. Many agreed that its charm was attributable precisely to this severity. Its solid stone had a unique coloration. At noon when the sun's rays ruled, the circle's stone looked pure white. When the setting sun sowed the horizon with dusk's rays, the ring's color changed and borrowed its hue from the flecks of gold on the Western horizon. When evening attacked and darkness settled over the desert, the collar also became gloomy, but the stone covering the mouth continued to glow mysteriously as if calling out to its devotees among the passersby or exchanging secret messages with the distant stars. During moonlit evenings, the ring would cheer up once more and regain its merry color.

But the patterning of the stone of the circular collar was even more beautiful.

The entire rim was marked with signs that ropes had cut into it over successive generations till these cuts in the smooth, translucent rock resembled the mark on the thighs of a camel or the deep scar of ancient wounds that time had healed. In this pattern, connoisseurs of the Unknown were wont to decipher signs of the time to come. It was said that diviners in the past had sought out the well—not to provision themselves with water—but to interrogate the stone and to research news of the time that had passed and of the time that was to come.

Over the course of the generations, many poems were recited in honor of the rim, and lovesick female poets still sing of it, comparing a lover known for faithful love to the rim of the well of Harakat. They have also used it as an epithet for patient people and added its name to every matter they wanted to characterize as immortal.

4

The tribe's strongest men dug in the northern passes; they dug in the lowlands of the southern plains; and they dug as well in sinkholes adjoining the valley bottoms to the west. Then they despaired. They dug down to great depths and reached great heights without even finding moist soil. So they despaired.

They gathered in the evening shadows and lowered their gaze as they normally did when despair gripped them. With their forefingers they imprinted riddles in the dirt. But they did not consult each other orally. They did not raise their voices in debate, because gloomy silence is always the language of despair. Proceeding a long way down the path of despair is an acknowledgement of the beauty of divestiture. Divestiture is the law that comes from the Unknown with inspiration, and inspiration was what reminded them of the excavator on one of those evenings.

They remembered the stranger who had lived with the tribe for many years with his only son; they had all joked—grown men, children, and women—about the satisfactions he found in the earth. He would say that the life above ground was a mistake for a man and that a wayfarer should not trust a place that provided no opportunity for him to crawl inside the belly of the earth. So he would lift his child down from behind his camel's hump whenever the tribe stopped traveling and decided to set up camp somewhere. Standing by the camel, he would unload from her the hoes, picks, and other stone implements that he had inherited from ancestors, who had used them as digging tools before the desert knew metals like copper and iron. Then he would stride around the area a little before choosing the suitable patch of ground to begin digging into. He would dig all day if the tribe reached the place early or dig all night long if the tribe arrived at a new site in the evening. He would dig without stopping until he had created in the belly of the earth a cave large enough to shelter him and his son. A portly man in his fourth or fifth decade, he was on the short side and wore a veil crowned with a protruding leather amulet. He encircled his belly with a thick leather girdle that extended from his ribcage to a little below his navel. Inquiring minds attributed the width of this belt to generous padding that the excavator had devised for a reason that the tribesmen only grasped the day a hostile tribe treacherously raided their encampment. Then they saw the excavator leap from his tomb beneath the earth and fight the enemies with pickaxes. When bowmen hit him with arrows, the belt deflected the blows. So he had real body armor. Then the people of the encampment knew for certain that the excavator had not adopted the broad belt, which was stuffed with straw and chaff, to help him dig, as he claimed. He had another secret reason. It was said that his strange habits dated back to an earlier period, when he married a young woman who was related to him. Then he dug an underground bed chamber for their wedding night, concealing the entrance under a blanket inside the bridal tent. He did not uncover it until the wedding officials left. At that time the naughty boys, who were accustomed to slip into the corners of tents to spy on couples on their wedding night, were flabbergasted when they saw the bride flee angrily from the tent. She reportedly said she wasn't a snake, a rat, or some ugly reptile to consent to live in a home underground. The excavator sent her a letter advising her that he had chosen to enter the dirt not only because he could find no place more secure than the earth but for its other qualities the tribe didn't know about. Then the bride unleashed the women poets on him. They recited deadly satires about his conduct; these were repeated by the beautiful women of neighboring tribes. But neither the satirical poems nor fear of disgrace could force the man to quit his subterranean chambers. Instead he became increasingly infatuated with this approach and dug even more. At times when the tribe settled on the earth for a long time, he made himself more than one dwelling. For her part, his bride never returned—perhaps because he made no effort to bring her back, perhaps because he never forgave her for her anger on their wedding night, and perhaps because he did not understand, or did not care to understand, what his fellows in the desert had grasped, namely that a woman is a tribulation acquired not only by renouncing pride but many other things as well.

His bride bore him a son before she disappeared from the desert in a lethal epidemic that harvested many members of the tribe. Then he took the child from the girl's family and introduced him to his excavations. He obtained from his clan two women slaves he had inherited from his ancestors—just as he had inherited his stone tools—to supervise rearing his child. Soon, however, he rid himself of them. He remarked that anyone who chose the earth's way and delivered his interests to the dirt would never need maids or slaves, and that caring for children even when they are quite young is less taxing than the headache of putting up with a hateful and ignoble community like that of servants. At first the tribeswomen pitied him. Later their pity turned into admiration. They would accost him and offer to help in disciplining the child, but the excavator would always thank them for their kindness and refuse their assistance with a politeness that women encountered only from hermits who had been secluded in desolate regions for long periods of time. It was said that he carried the child on his back in a rope halter when he went out to search for his camels, to gather firewood, or to collect truffles. It was said that he knew how to hide him from sight in high mountain crevices or in a hole the mouth of which only he could find. It was also said that he had taken a captivating bride who was one of the women of the Spirit World and that she took charge of the child for him. Many swore by the mightiest gods of the desert that they had repeatedly seen him in the company of this beauty on his wanderings but that she would disappear and vanish when they drew near. Others spoke of hearing him with their own ears converse with this female jinni; they had not, however, discerned her body or seen any figure.

5

The earth spoke to him.

The earth spoke to him; so he did not cast an eye toward the sky.

He had not gazed at the sky since he emerged from inside the tent and crawled across the earth to the distant pastures. On the trail to the pastures, he heard her speak for the first time. She spoke through the stone stelae. She spoke to him through the trunks of acacias enveloped in the evening's gloom. She spoke to him through retem blossoms that bowl people over with their fragrance, which fills breasts with ecstasy, dizziness, and longing. She spoke to him through the summits of northern mountains that are clad in turbans of celestial fabric threaded with color from dawn's firebrand. She spoke through grim expanses of the wasteland, which coaxes the wanderer till he yields, gives away everything, and advances when she leads him down the path to the Unknown, from which he never turns back. She spoke to him through the stillness of the nights, the empty expanses of which were dominated by flooding moonlight. She would humble herself, withdraw, and divest herself as if she were chief of all insouciant creatures.

She spoke to him in many tongues. Then he understood, and the mysterious firebrand overwhelmed him. He wept and prostrated himself, hearing nothing but her whispering and seeing nothing but her body since that day long ago.

After that, the sky fled from the sky and on earth only the earth remained.

6

Who had told him in times forgotten that the earth is the appropriate abode? Was it his father, whom he didn't remember? Was it the tribe's leader long ago? Was it the voice of the ancestors? Was it a messenger from the inhabitants of the Spirit World? Or, was it the earth herself who had communicated with a mysterious cry, confiding to him that she is a mother who must never be forsaken?

In that period—the days of childhood, play, and innocence—the earth was very close. He would crawl outside to play between the tent sites, plunge into her dirt and clay, and smear his face with her sand. He was only inches from her breast and stumbled on all fours across her palm. He would stand only to fall the next instant. When he pushed up even as high as a knuckle, he would be seized by fear—a nameless, noble fear imbued with a sense of danger. Was it the danger of falling? The danger of leaving never to return? The danger of the first step on the path to the labyrinth? Or, was it the enigmatic sensation of being on the verge of losing paradise and the voice of the herald crying that the time is nigh for a migration from which there is no return?

But the trip does not begin blindly, because the enigmatic desert does not allow its children to depart without instructions. The lesson begins with the first step. Then the little wanderer meets its prophecies in the plasticity of the clay he molds, in the scraggly plants the desert produces bountifully in rainy seasons, in the tiny grains it slips into the bread dough that its sands cook. Afterwards it leads him by the hand on another journey. It takes him on a tour of the grazing lands to teach him the trails that lead out of them. On the naked plains it lashes him with winds that strike the faces of wanderers with grit. Or, it frowns, glowers, and pours down a deluge of rain. Or, it exhales feverish fire in the seasons of the Qibli wind. Or, it unleashes cold in winter seasons. It employs many strategies to inform the young wanderer that the migratory route will be desolate and inescapable if he does not rely on her, if he is not guided by her, and if he does not remain loyal to her. So he realizes and learns from the first day that in this tenebrous, munificent terrain, which extends and renews itself forever, there is a secret he can never dispense with. In it lurks that cryptic amulet the traveler in the labyrinth can never do without.

7

When the messenger from the nobles arrived that evening, he was recalling his life story and hiding out in his cellar. He was recalling this amulet, because he—unlike the others—had never forgotten it. He hadn't forgotten it, because the mother hadn't shared it with him during that forgotten time of innocence when she had told the others. He hadn't forgotten it because the earth screamed advice in his ear the way desert mothers normally scream the names of newborn babes in their ears. Perhaps for this reason he hadn't followed the same path the others had in their migrations. The others had pursued the trail toward the horizon, whereas he had followed the trail leading to the depths. His mates had set out, like those before them, on the path of the extensive wasteland. He, on the other hand, had bowed his head, looked down into the belly, and established his dwelling inside its breast before building his vaults in the dirt, fleeing from the labyrinth of the expanse, while seeking protection with the mother from the ghoul of loss.

He was reliving his life when the messenger of the elders visited him.

He normally recalled that story every day—indeed, several times a day, because the mother to whose breast he had come for refuge would repeat her counsels to him, lest he forget, and deliver new instructions on each occasion. He would eavesdrop and hear this female diviner when she mocked her naughty children who had fled and raced into the wasteland, lured by the horizons. They capitulated, darted off, and then rolled around the way tumbleweed does when the wind drives it. They forgot the lower reaches just as quickly as they forgot her counsels. Then they considered vain locomotion to be a homeland, and the search scorched them with fires of longing. So they rushed off, and the fates of the primeval labyrinth changed into genuine and lethal loss.

Since he was listening carefully, he heard their footsteps from his shelter. They were pounding on the earth as if they wanted to harm it. They exaggerated their boorishness as if they deliberately wanted to cave the earth into the earth, without planning an escape route should the earth sink and flee from the earth. They were wandering aimlessly over her face like the hoi polloi, who don't know what they are doing, don't fathom where they are going, and don't understand what they want.

He was hunkered down in the earth, hearing, listening, brooding, wondering, and becoming ever more certain that salvation is possible only through proceeding farther down the corridor and digging deeper into the belly of the earth.

They ridiculed his shelter, but their ridicule only made him more convinced. The female poets satirized him, but he laughed at their verses in his subterranean vaults and smiled from ear to ear. Once he committed an error. He chased after the beauty and had a child by her. But he decided to atone for his sin. So he taught the child the counsels of the lower reaches, of isolation, and of stillness. The baby was only calm when he brought him into the shelter and placed him as a pledge in the hand of the earth.

8

In the council he leaned forward over his homeland and read in its skin the dirt's riddles. They told him they had dug, searched, and torn the body of the earth until they had despaired. They also said that they had finally learned that they would never find a way to water if he did not come to their aid. So would the son of the earth countenance the people of the earth or would he reject them and disappoint their request?

He leaned further forward. He bowed so low that his bent head touched his chest while his fingers continued to trace a sign in the earth's book. He dug furrows with his forefinger and with all his fingers punched the tracks of various creatures: the pawing of a camel's hoof, the imprint of a jackal, the trudging of dung beetles, and the twisting trail of the snake.

Aggulli said, "The well on the mountain slope destroyed us. We have excavated many summits without even reaching damp soil. What does this mean?"

He stopped making tracks in the earth and extended the tips of his fingers to gather some pebbles—white, gray, black, and gold ones. He constructed a small pile with them—a mass that was approximately level. Then he began to remove the colored stones from the pile and drew some signs near it.

Imaswan Wandarran explained, "Had it not been for the prophecy, we would not have needed all this. You know that we haven't settled on the earth in response to some whim; it is what the leader willed. Since we have resigned ourselves to remaining in this place, we must find water to serve us as a consolation and a peg. The presence among us of a man who knows the depths of the earth as well as he knows the ends of his fingers has escaped us throughout our search. So did we err in sending for you?"

He arranged the golden pebbles in a vertical column, which he traversed with a chain of black stones. Then the beautiful intersection was visible: the sign of the goddess Tanit.

The hero intervened for the first time, "Our reliance on this earth benefits our venerable companion. From today forward you won't need to leave your refuge here to dig another one there. Do you take my point?"

The excavator glanced stealthily at Ahallum. A flash gleamed in his stern eyes, but he bent over the mandala again. He chose white stones from the pile and arranged them around the upper part of the cross. Then he encircled the lower part of the figure with the gray pebbles. The circle around the cross was divided into two colors, and the first figure was split into four triangles. The triangle is also a symbol of the goddess Tanit. Emmamma interjected a comment from another angle. He spoke swaying like those possessed. Before he spoke, he sang that tuneful moan that the people of the wasteland are accustomed to hear from noble elders who have inhabited eternity for long periods till nothing of them remains in this world save their scrawny bodies.

He said, "Loath as we are to send for a man to teach us to dig pits, the ancients taught us to search for the secret of something before beginning to search for it. All of us know that the desert, like the sky, conceals in its belly a secret bigger than all the treasures that have captivated the minds of greedy people from antiquity. We have also inherited from the first peoples the insight that the earth's secret is one of the secrets of the desert. If the sages had not hovered around its secret for ages, they would not have been able to discover the Law."

He set about buttressing his statement by proof-texting it from provisos of the Law while his meager body swayed right and left. He chanted a moan that almost evolved into the tune of a sorrowful ballad. Then he spoke once more, saying that their companion was the man closest to the earth, because things reveal their secrets only to one who loves them and offers them not only an attentive ear but goes farther and commits his affairs to them. Finally he ended by saying, "We have come to you hoping you will tell us the secret."

Silence prevailed. His fingers stopped arranging the pebbles.

Aggulli repeated, "We have come to you hoping you will tell us the secret."

They all repeated this statement in unison. They repeated the statement as if reciting one of the talismans of the first peoples.

9

"I must admit there is a secret to this." He repeated that twice, just as they had twice repeated the venerable elder's talisman in unison. He looked up at them for the first time, and they noticed traces of a sparkle, ecstasy, and tears in his eyes.

He declared definitively, "A sacrifice!"

They exchanged astonished looks before asking, "Sacrifice?"

He glanced boldly from one to another of them, and the amulet attached to the front of his veil at the top seemed to protrude and move higher. He repeated this prophecy: "A sacrifice!"

Aggulli protested, "But we slaughtered a sacrificial victim on day one!"

Then the excavator's body was seized by the fever of ecstatics, and the tears in his eyes became clearly visible. He released a long moan like those of Emmamma when the venerable elder sang sad songs from the desert of eternity. Trembling overwhelmed him, and he swayed and shook. He tried to calm his longing and returned to his sacred mandala, but his fingers betrayed him. When he picked up a pebble it would fall before he could place it in an empty spot in the figure. He shook the dirt from his hands and ran his right hand over his broad leather girdle. He sighed emotionally and asked, "What do you know about sacrificial victims? What do you know about the earth? If you slaughter a black goat to extract a little gold dust, should you slaughter a black goat when you wish to extract water? Don't you realize you're disparaging the earth's treasure, the truth's treasure, when you offer the same sacrificial kid for both of these treasures, even though people think it a major sin to compare the two?"

The elders exchanged questioning glances, and their fingers stopped fiddling in the dirt. Aggulli observed, "The truth is that we've never dug a well before. How would we know what blood offering the earth demands as the price for water?"

"Before we speak of the blood offering, let's discuss the location. I've heard where you've dug and know that you missed the right place. Don't you realize that the earth is a body comparable to that of a slaughtered animal? Haven't you seen how a skillful butcher will follow the joints when butchering a carcass? Don't you know that the belly of the earth also has articulations and that water flows through the lower reaches of the earth like blood flowing through bodies?"

Imaswan Wandarran cried out, "You all see? Didn't I tell you we didn't pick the right place even once?"

The excavator paid him no heed. He cast a look all around the council. Then he said, "Earth's blood is water; nothing demands a blood offering so much as blood. Nothing on earth seeks the blood of a sacrificial victim as much as blood!"

He bent over his mandala again and dropped a pebble to fill a gap in the right triangle on the upper edge. He repeated his prophecy as if reading it from a symbol in the sacred mandala: "Nothing on earth seeks the blood of a sacrificial victim as much as blood!"

Aggulli asked, "Do you want us to slaughter a whole herd? Would the blood of a herd suffice to obtain water?"

"A herd's blood is an appropriate offering for evanescent treasures."

"Into which group of blood offerings does water fall?" He looked up mournfully at their guest.

The excavator replied almost in a whisper, "Water bears no relationship to your blood offerings. Water isn't a transient treasure. Water is another type of being."

"Tell us a little about water!"

"Can a creature like me speak of water? I admit that I have spent long years with it; but I can't claim to understand water."

"Do you want us to believe that a boon companion knows nothing of his friend of many years?"

"I acknowledge that the earth's compassion has been greater than I could ever have imagined. Water has come to me as a messenger and kept me company in my solitude."

"What does water say? Tell us what water has confided to you."

He raised his head high, and the leather amulet attached to the front of his veil shot up. Then he leaned toward Aggulli till the amulet almost touched his companion's veil. His eyes narrowed to slits. He replied in a mysterious voice, "The earth's tongue can only be understood by someone who lives in the earth. Only someone who has lost the ability to use people's language comprehends water's language."

Silence reigned. Eventually Emmamma's voice rose in a sorrowful moan. Ahallum interjected, "Let's go back to the blood offering!"

More than one voice seconded his suggestion. Then the excavator asked, "Remember the blood sacrifice for the sky's water?"

They kept still for a long time. Then Aggulli asked suspiciously, "What are you saying?"

"I'm saying that the sky took the tribe's soothsayer as the price for the sky's water."

The nobles exchanged glances again. Aggulli asked even more skeptically, "What are you saying?"

The excavator dropped more stones into the column dividing the circle. The column was duplicated, leaving the design unbalanced. He lined up other pebbles along the horizontal line to restore the mandala's balance. Without looking up, he replied, "I'm saying that the earth's water is just as dear as the sky's."

The elders observed him with suspicious eyes as Aggulli resumed his questioning: "What are you saying?"

"I mean to say that the earth's sacrificial victim will be no less significant than the sky's!"

A grumbling murmur was audible in the council, and the excavator leapt to his feet.

1 0

Ever since he had learned how to excavate and had discovered his first drop of water inside the earth's cavity, he had asked this messenger whence it came and where it was heading. At first it oozed from clefts in rocks—viscous, skimpy, and mysterious. He would run his fingers over the smooth slabs to feel the moist viscosity. He would lick the ends of his fingers with the tip of his tongue, savoring the salinity, the array of metals, the mix of soils, and the sweetness of the torrents' waters in turn. The secret of this unidentified messenger, however, grew increasingly obscure during a migration.

In some places he found no trace of it but would hear its melodies once he had finished digging his shelter and stretched out to sleep. Then he would press against the earth, pulling the encircling blanket's edge from his lower ear, and listen. At times, while listening, he would hear a distant, unruly roar. At other times he would hear an obscure, insistent chatter. Eventually, he learned something about the modus operandi of this messenger, which would growl when raging and rush away as if falling from an abyss. It hid in aquifers as if fleeing from a jinni afreet. It raced migrating nomads and beat them to an earth that does not exist on earth. It would sing during its eternal journey the hostile rap song that does not so much reveal as conceal a secret. The excavator followed the song and discovered its moist tongue. Torments of longing would overwhelm him, and he would not even be aware of the tears welling up in his eyes. He would not hear himself addressing this nomad with a nomad's language: "Where do you come from, Water? Where are you heading, Water?" At times when the subterranean currents slowed, as he delighted in this traveler's murky chatter, he understood his beloved was busy addressing creatures. These addresses were muffled but amiable and eager, and contained in their tunes the angst of lovers.

He would follow these arcane orations till he forgot himself. The tongue would engross him, and the messenger's prophecies would seize hold of him. The creatures' replies would also astonish him. The soirée would continue with diverting evening conversation, and he would quit the earth as astonishment at the talisman overcame him. He would repeat it as a mantra for reflection. Then a glow would lead him to the door of riddles. So he would be amazed, laugh out loud, question, explore, or doze off. By keeping tabs on the question, he would find solace and attain the life normally lost through sociability, which he considered a catnap.

He would have liked not to return from this slumber. He hoped he would not be forced to pry his ear from the earth. He would rather not have been obliged to stand on his feet. He hoped he wouldn't emerge from the subterranean corridor's dark recesses. He frequently remained beneath the lower levels for entire days, coming out only when the sages worried about his absence and came to intrude on his solitude in the shelter.

But departure also had a set date, and the hour of farewell would inevitably arrive one day. The herald would rush through the wasteland, crying out the day of their departure. Tumult would dominate the campsite, boys would race between tent sites, women would emerge to break down the tents, herdsmen would arrive with the caravans of camels, and slaves, servants, and vassals would start readying the bags and cinching up the luggage. Then he would descend.

He would descend to the lower reaches, pull the corner of the blanket away from his right ear, and prostrate himself. He would press himself against the dirt, stretch out, lie on his belly, and touch his lips to the clay. Then the salty crystals would slide into his mouth and onto his tongue as he sensed the delicious saline taste. He would press more firmly against the body and meld with it till he became the groom uniting with his bride on their wedding night. He would tremble and shudder, overwhelmed by an orgasmic climax. Then the eternal melody would break out from the solid rock. The song would grow louder and flow through the earth's body before circulating through his whole physique. He would hear the eternal call, and longing would flood out and subdue the world of sorrows. He would mumble impotently, "Master, may I accompany you? Why don't you take me with you, God of Wanderers?" The call would grow more intense; the leitmotif of sorrow would become more strident in the call, and tears would spring from his eyes while his breast heaved with groans of lamentation. Then the leader's messengers would arrive to wrench him forcibly away from this feverish tryst.

11

"Master, may I accompany you? Why don't you take me with you, God of Wanderers?"

He repeated this talisman to himself at first in secret. Then he uttered it in public. Next he sang the call once he found the articulated joint and began to strike the earth with a terrifying stone-headed pickaxe.

At first, boys gathered around him, but the elders soon arrived.

They arrived as if coming for a council meeting. The venerable elder led the way, but bursts of wind buffeted his skinny body, which lurched with the gusts. So he would swerve off the path for some steps. The group behind him veered off course, too, without ever offering to assist him. When he returned to the trail, they returned also, still walking behind him. He brandished his burnished stick in the empty air and emitted the groans of people who have lived for a long time, who have lost their contemporaries, who have lost their loved ones, and who wander through tribes like strangers.

The venerable elder stood above him and gazed at the void, which was flooded with mirage trails. His beady eyes stared at the expanse that everyone knew he couldn't see, because eyes accustomed to gazing at the homelands of eternity cannot revert to viewing the wasteland of the living.

He emitted his painful moan, the moan of the defenseless, the moan of exiles, the moan of people who have crossed with those who have traveled back into antiquity, leaving behind in the desert only their scrawny bodies. To the excavator's ears, this moan sounded like another wail of lament.

Emmamma uttered his prophecy from the other shore: "I was sure you would attempt to find the secret. I was certain that water is a treasure only found by a man with a talisman."

The men removed their flowing garments, rolled up their sleeves, cinched their belts tight, and began to dig.

1 2

That night he heard the call.

He went to sleep and a little later heard the call. He did not exactly hear the call that night; instead he made the rounds with the wanderer, tasting the pleasure of sliding along, flowing past like the days, and losing spatial limitations once he discovered he was every place. When he awoke from his slumbers, he heard the messenger's chattering clearly. He heard the messenger dancing with the outcroppings of solid rock, getting cheeky with slabs of stone, dispersing in hollows in the lowlands, complaining for a time, then clamoring, and jabbering in some other language occasionally. The messenger fell, frothed, leveled off, bubbled up, and flowed through the secret articulations, racing against the march of days without the days' dominion realizing it. The messenger told the creatures of the lower reaches about the pit. It said it came as a messenger from the sky to become the earth's blood, the earth's tongue, the earth's spirit, and the earth's call. It wasn't shy about revealing the secret and telling creatures of the lower reaches that it is the call. It addressed its loved ones only allegorically, but the creatures heard the word "call" as clearly as those inhabiting the nugatory realm. Then some factions believed what they heard and others denied it.

1 3

That night he woke the boy.

He woke him and spoke to him in the darkness—the darkness of his grotto and the darkness outside.

The boy wiped his eyes with his hands and protested audibly.

The man addressed him, saying, "I have frequently spoken to you about migration. Do you remember what I have said?"

The boy continued to rub his eyes, face, and head with his hands, struggling to stay awake. He murmured something indecipherable but did not speak.

The man said to him, "I told you that we don't come to the desert to rest on the desert. Instead each of us comes to chase after the others in the wasteland like the tails of mirages. The adult outstrips the youth, but the lucky person outstrips everyone else and departs while still a child in the cradle."

The boy did not respond. So the man continued, "There is a small faction who burden the earth and only emerge when they hear the call."

The child stopped messing with parts of his body and exclaimed in a weird voice, "The call?"

"The call. The call is a present from the sky. The call is the language of the earth. The call is the gift of the possessed."

The boy was still. He soon muttered, "Did Amghar refer to the possessed?"[11]

"Yes, Amghar is speaking about the possessed, because possessed people are additional conduits. The possessed are another community. For this reason, a possessed person shouldn't tarry when he hears the call."

". . . ."

"This is why I woke you. This is why I want to tell you that my time has come and that my call is ringing in my ears night and day. So promise me that you'll be true to the covenant and that you'll never abandon your mother, the earth."

The boy mumbled indistinctly. The father made himself clearer with a decisive phrase: "Beware of fleeing the earth. You should know you'll never get far if you do!"

". . . ."

"I bequeath you the pickaxe. Beware of going too far away."

The son yawned loudly, and so the father fell silent. The boy leaned forward and fell asleep. The father dozed off as the call resounded in his ears.

14

Weeping woke him several hours later that night.

He rose to find his son collapsed in a heap beside him, weeping loudly. He felt like questioning him but decided to refrain and then fell asleep again. The boy wept till morning. Then he went out to the plain, still weeping. He accompanied the herdsmen when they departed to

---

11. Tamasheq for father, grandfather, tribal elder, or leader.

the pastures. Since he was weeping, they asked, "Why are you crying?" But he didn't reply. He left the herders and returned to wander among the dwellings.

The sages stopped him and asked, "Why are you weeping?" He did not reply. Instead he hid his face in his arms and walked away. The women went to him and also asked about the secret cause of his weeping. He did not answer them either. Then his chums blocked his way and questioned him. They asked persistently, but he crossed the vacant land to the heights to the north and roamed there for a long time.

The tribe grasped the secret behind his weeping some days later.

15

The nobles led their assistants, vassals, and slaves to the well as if they were the tribe's heroes leading mounted warriors on a raid.

They trailed across the low-lying, vacant land south of the temple. Then they took turns descending down the shaft, their belts lashed securely with palm-fiber ropes. They dug the pit deeper and reached moist earth after penetrating a few cubits farther down.

The excavator struck the blow that cut through to the moisture. He took the hunk of damp clay in his hands and tasted it with his tongue. He closed his eyes and savored the morsel, leaning to the left and right. He emitted a groan of approval. Then he shared the good news with the people: "I bet there'll be a greater consensus among you about the sweetness of the water than about anything in your lives ever!"

The depths resounded with the call of the depths, but the people above ground did not make out the words clearly. One man shouted a question down the shaft. So the excavator placed a lump of the clay in the container hanging over his head and jerked on the rope that hung there to signal for them to begin pulling it up. They drew the bucket up and struggled with each other for the moist clay. He heard them express their delight, shout to each other, and argue with one another as they exchanged muddy handfuls of the treasure.

He bent over and splintered the hard place with the solid stone of his alarming pickaxe. The earth at the bottom of the pit was astonishing. In its dirt, pebbles and pieces of white stone mixed with thin slabs of stone and promising lumps of clay. He dug at the heart of the pit for a time but

found it was less moist there. So he turned his attention to the west side
and struck the earth from there. He struck once, twice, three times. Then,
after this final blow, the Master flowed out. It trickled from a fissure on
the right side. It seeped from the pores of a solid, snowy white slab, which
began to sweat. Then this perspiration dripped down, and beads of
sweat collected on the august, generous body that darkness had hidden
from the human eye forever. These beads increased in circumference,
plumpness, and size. He dragged the blade of his pickaxe along the
indescribable fissure. Then stone pummeled stone, and the solid rock
spoke with a hushed voice. From the talk of the solid rock was born an
actual being. The deluge flooded out and gushed down in a succession of
large drops. In no time at all, the drops united in a line that continued to
bleed, bleed, bleed. It bled and spoke as it fell on the rocks at the bottom.
The wanderer saw it for the first time and heard its whisper like the first
gasp of a newborn child.

1 6

He watched the wanderer change and evolve into a truly heavenly stream.
He watched the mysterious wanderer emerge from the Unknown as a
body. He watched the immortal wanderer collect, take shape, multiply,
and appropriate a fluent, running tongue.

He watched the miracle jabber, flood, inundate the rocks, and rise to
form a circular pond on which the light of the well's mouth fell. Then it
shone with a glimmering, dreadfully seductive charm.

The pulsing deluge damaged the hastily done work. Then the liquid
poured from the groins of the fissure, and the pores of the rocks secreted
even more. The creature twisted as it traveled and crossed on its eternal
trip to the valley bottoms. So the disciple witnessed in its passage the
secret of the Master and the birth of primeval life.

The heartbeat increased, and the anguish of the first people assailed
him. Then he wailed, "May I accompany you, Master? Why don't you
carry us along on the journey, God of Wanderers?" Then a tremor struck
that patch of ground.

The people above heard the earthquake, and the ground trembled
violently beneath their feet. They shoved forward to the chasm. They
leaned over its opening and batted away the spray that wet their

downturned faces. This spray was thick, viscous, heavy, and mixed with mud, dirt, and gravel. They saw that surging water had risen to the top. They realized that an internal collapse had narrowed the well's shaft and pushed the water up. They called to one another, fastened palm-fiber belts to their bodies, and were quick to dangle down the well, taking pickaxes and leather containers designed to haul dirt from wells. Three men descended and began filling the containers with lumps of clay, mud, and dirt. They immediately tugged on the rope when they finished filling the leather buckets. The other strongest men collaborated above at the mouth. The men unloaded a lot of dirt and kept drawing out containers of it all day long. But they only reached the buried man shortly before sunset.

Aggulli reached him. He found him tucked beneath an awe-inspiring slab of white stone that was marked on the underside with arcane lines like a sorcerer's symbols. It was bisected by a network of minute veins that antiquity had traced inside the slab. Perhaps the pranks of some mysterious creature had dug them, one generation after another, till it became an indecipherable legacy like the talismans of the first peoples carved into walls of caves. He cautiously lifted the slab away and raised the excavator's head. The lower part of his veil was missing, and his gray beard, coated with mud mixed with pebbles, was smeared with clay. There was an enigmatic smile on his lips, and his eyes expressed profound acquiescence. The blood flowing freely from his forehead mixed with lines from the rogue flood. Even after the victim was pulled out, his bleeding continued. Blood flowed from his forehead, deluged his face, eyes, lips, and beard, and fell to mingle with the deluge in the pit of the well.

Aggulli embraced him for a long time. He continued hugging him even after he wrapped the dread rope carefully around both their bodies. He tugged hard on the rope to sanction the start of their ascent.

The strongest men stepped forward to pull them up. When they reached the mouth, the bond was unfastened in dignified silence. Aggulli too was all bloody. Blood covered his face and arms and stained all his clothes. The men noticed his eyes' redness, gleam, and tears. They shrouded the deceased man near the mouth of the well, and then Aggulli fled to the wasteland.

Emmamma approached.

He stood over the drowned man and stared at the horizon, which was flooded with dusk's rays. His beady eyes stared, and then he released a distressing moan like a lament. Finally he said, "I knew he would go before us. I knew the verbal secret would not suffice to obtain water. I knew that blood is the price of blood."

He began his wailing lament again. Then many people remembered the son's wails and realized that the boy's weeping had been a prophecy.

XIV

NEW WAW

There was an ancient city that settlers from Tyre held.

Virgil, *The Aeneid*, I, 12

1

During the first years, water gushed from the well nonstop.

The tribe was upset that water was going to waste, and the sages tried to prevent the water from flowing away. They built a sturdy cistern at the spring's outlet and channeled the overflow between chunks of rock and dams of stones. They allowed neighboring tribes to fetch all the water they needed and set fees for herdsmen who preferred to bring their camels and livestock to this well rather than travel to distant wells in the Western and Central Hammada. Even so, the large daily discharge of water—the deluge they had sought for so long and for which they had offered mighty sacrifices—exceeded the tribe's needs and those of the neighboring tribes. The water rebelled against their dams, overtopped the cisterns and confinement pools, continued to flow in small streams down the slopes, watering the lowlands separating the well from Retem Valley, and flooded tracts covered with a layer of clay in some places and topped with smooth pebbles in others. Then it descended into the valley, down a low shoulder where the valley's sides spread out. So the watercourse expanded there, the stream's banks spread far apart, and the water grew shallow.

In the first periods, thirst was conquered, and the soil swallowed the water and stored some in pools the way it usually did in seasons of transient rains. As the water continued to flow, however, it finally succeeded in transforming the earth's behavior. Then the retem trees at the bottom of the valley grew greener, and their flowers perfumed all the surrounding desert. Dense undergrowth sprouted between these trees, and the valley was dominated by groves and a forest that extended for a long way. The plateau lying between the mouth of the well and the lip of the valley was also transformed. In the early years, amazing wild plants grew there, coloring all the expanses of land with beautiful carpets. The colors of the flowers that rose from the grass divided these green carpets into sections colored by the flowers. At first it was grazing land frequented by young herders, but herbalists quickly discovered the qualities of the plants and began to pick herbs to use in their mysterious potions.

Later, the sages realized the necessity of utilizing the deluge that was being lost in the open countryside. So they planted wheat and barley and imported from the Southern oases palm seedlings to plant. Their delight was enormous when the plants started bearing fruit the first year. The boughs of the young palms sank under the weight of the most delicious types of dates, and before the end of that season they had eaten genuine ripe, fresh dates—just like inhabitants of the oases.

During subsequent years, the palms rose high, and the pomegranate and fig trees matured. They planted vegetables too and harvested cereal crops, acquiring a surplus that they exchanged with the caravan merchants at exorbitant prices.

The desolate, dead, bare tract of land was transformed into a garden that voyagers could see from great distances. Despite this bounty, the new oasis did not experience prosperity and did not enjoy its golden age until commercial caravans discovered it and changed their former routes. Then the oasis was transformed in a short time into a commercial hub, where caravans coming from all directions met.

2

In the early days they gathered stones to build widely separated houses, constructing the walls deliberately, skeptically, and hesitantly, but their souls' doubts, which at the outset had stifled any excitement, quickly evolved into a spirit of competition. Then they went to great pains to build at a faster pace. So the plateaus and the string of low-lying areas to the north were dotted with buildings, and these subsequently spread to the plain of the central depression. They also extended west until they overlooked clay-covered earth that was bare of any gravel or boulders and that rain flooded in the winter. Southern breezes generously blew top soil from the badlands over these areas so tender shoots of plants grew plentifully in the spring and the plains turned green. Then the girls went out to harvest the abundant truffles, although herdsmen commented that there were fewer truffles in the fields at the borders of the encampments compared to their plentiful numbers in western sites at greater distances from the dwellings.

In the beginning, anarchy was a hallmark of the construction and placement of houses; random spacing, crowding, and separation were blatantly obvious. This did not escape the notice of anyone who saw them—not even visitors. With the passage of time, however, the city plan became more orderly. Houses were packed together, walls abutted each other as the buildings clung together, and external walls united with each other. Then roads and lanes were established between the dwellings, and blocks of buildings were separated by streets, alleys, and paths. The streets led to plazas and open spaces in the midst of the crush of buildings. Artisans, blacksmiths, farmers, and camel herders arrived and turned empty areas into markets for buying, selling, and bartering. The alleyways were narrow and winding, but the sages of the oasis understood that the winding streets and narrow alleys were a legacy of the chaotic construction boom of the first years.

The use of gray tones—borrowed from the darkness of the neighboring landscape and adopted by the house walls—dated back to that era. In due time, however, the tribe acquired the strategies of civil strife and learned the arts of embellishment and decoration, because rock continued to be a stubborn medium. Then the tribe discovered white lime powder and covered walls with this blinding white color. Then smooth walls gleamed in the morning sun, and in that grim, gray countryside the oasis appeared to the eye of the passing traveler to be an amazing city of the jinn or a unique oasis belonging to the group of lost oases celebrated in the legends of the ancients and said to appear only to travelers who are not looking for them, since they disappear from view when approached by people who have left home in search of them.

3

To the east of the hill where the tomb stood, a short street led to a plaza surrounded by rows of tall buildings. The bottom floors of these were open spaces that smiths had adopted as workshops for hammering metals and forging blades, knives, swords, spears, arrows, and utilitarian items for daily use. On the other side of the temple, skilled craftsmen and artisans were grouped. They prepared their infernal kilns and began to fire pottery, providing the tribesmen with earthenware jugs, pots for cooking, and other containers suitable for a sedentary population— instead of their old-fashioned wooden vessels.

The market for general merchandise occupied the center of the oasis on the south. This open area, which lay parallel to the well on the west, was now threatened by urban sprawl and the aggressive building boom. Earlier it had been a pasture for their herds and a savannah covered with acacia trees.

Caravans converged here from every direction. Those from the South brought loads of dates and palm products like palm-fiber rope, sacks woven from this fiber, platters made of palm fronds, and logs of palm trunks to be used in building roofs. Caravans from the Southern forests brought back cargoes of gold dust, ostrich feathers, elephant tusks, and the hides of wild animals. From the North came caravans bringing grains, oils, textiles, and some items made of metal. In the oasis market, goods were exchanged and barters concluded. Commerce's feverish infection spread to the inhabitants, who avidly initiated heated negotiations. Then merchants formed alliances or revived old friendships that had been sacrificed to the pursuit of gold dust. So they convened around tables laden with food and concluded with fellow merchants deals that their renewed pursuit of wealth would soon infect with the plague called forgetfulness. All the same, they would never tire of striking new deals when they chanced to meet in the markets.

Caravans stocked up on water and supplies in the oasis. Frequently pack animals were relieved of their loads of merchandise or at least their burdens were lightened. Other caravans meanwhile sought to increase their loads with other goods. During its years of prosperity, caravans made their way to the oasis from the North, South, and West to buy goods from its markets, which were richly stocked with the most precious items. They took advantage of its proximity, plentiful water, low tax rates, and its markets' ample supply of even the rarest merchandise. Older merchants would frequently observe with amazement to one another, "We passed by this spot repeatedly and found it a harsh, deadly wasteland. After seeing it now, how could we dare claim that heaven has grown stingy with its miracles? Doesn't this mean that when the Spirit World looks favorably on a lineage, it creates wealth from nothing?"

4

These commercial caravans had brought many people to the oasis since its first years. Some came to seek their fortune, and others arrived en route to other destinations but were tempted by the land and bonded with the newly born oasis because of the alluring opportunities provided by its development. So they deemed it a promising location and settled there. A third group consisted of world travelers and adventurers who roved the deserts from wanderlust, fleeing from rumors about them and attempting to lose themselves in foreign realms. They hoped that luck would smile on them and that one day they would discover their true potential.

Artisans, merchants, women entertainers, and tramps settled in the oasis. At first they resided in its only guesthouse. Then they leased houses in the more frequented alleys. Over time some immigrants started to adopt alien ways and formed gangs and cliques that through their conduct and character soon provoked the original inhabitants. Then disputes broke out, rivalries were spawned, and the wick of civil disturbance was lit. Citizens complained and brought the matter to the Council. Its nobles met in the one building erected on the hill to the west of the mausoleum. They consulted with each other, debated with each other, and disagreed with each other. The first faction alleged that the foreigners had introduced weird heresies to the land and that the tribe would eventually realize the danger, because these violated the Law and threatened to pollute the inhabitants, whose souls' purity would be destroyed in the near future. This faction advocated cleansing the oasis of the contamination by expelling these intruders at the earliest opportunity. The second faction considered the droves of immigrants to be an asset for the tribe and a benefit that no burgeoning oasis could dispense with. They observed that most of the new arrivals were craftsmen, skilled workmen, and artisans. Therefore markets in the oasis would benefit greatly from their influx, which would certainly spur the development of crafts, create jobs, and invigorate life in the oasis.

When the consultative assembly did not reach a consensus, the sages recommended recourse to the mausoleum. There they raised with the female diviner the issue of the fate of the foreign migrants. The Virgin rested her head on the stones all night long; in the morning she sent the leaders the following dictum: "There is no good in a land that the feet of foreigners have not trod." The nobles repeated this inspired dictum with all the solemnity due a prophecy. They recited this talisman to themselves before seeking out representatives of the immigrants to share this good news with them.

5

The immigrants acquired the right to stay in the oasis in exchange for payment of a regular poll tax. Laws were drafted to formalize their relations with the original inhabitants. These imposed on immigrants respect for the customary laws of the oasis and deference to the dictates of the Law. Immigrants were forbidden from interfering with classified matters that related only to the original inhabitants. The most common infraction, however, and one that always led to the expulsion of the alien from the oasis, was a violation of the ancient prohibition against transactions conducted in gold and the possession of gold coins. In a matter of days, civil guards were seen leading a foreigner outside the walls of the oasis after he was charged with possession of the ill-omened metal, even though the laws stipulated that a verdict of exile against such individuals could not be executed until solemn testimony from sound-minded eyewitnesses was obtained.

It was said that trade with this sinister metal constituted the one ban that most weakened the immigrant community. The tribesmen mocked them and derided their fondness for a metal that differed from others solely by its spurious luster. The foreigners rebutted this charge, arguing that the sages of the oasis had imposed on them a debilitating condition that human beings could not endure, because they belonged to nations that had no known criterion for prosperity or engine for life besides gold. They themselves had migrated, sacrificed their former lives in their homelands, and rushed off to spread around the world expressly in a quest for gold. How could jurists require them to renounce a goal that was their sole reason for leaving their homes? Or were the nobles stipulating this to undercut the prophecy and to take back from immigrants with their left hand what the leader had granted them with his right one?

6

No sooner had the decision been made to construct walls around the community than a new dispute flared up in the Council of Nobles. The sages would not have countenanced criticism of the benefits of walls if the person lodging the protest had not been the venerable elder. He was reported to have declared that the walls of oases in which brave men live should not be composed of blocks of stones and lumps of clay; they should instead consist of the blades of swords and points of spears. Many agreed with him that walls provide no protection for cowardly, servile, and feeble people, even if built of iron plates, and that the only reliable safeguard for nations and rebuff for aggressors is the vigilance of their mounted warriors. The majority, however, spoke about the need for walls and for block-and-mortar construction of an all-encompassing oasis wall. They affirmed that these physical constructions would not be a substitute for sword blades, because nations don't build walls as an indictment of the bravery of their warriors but rather as an extra precaution to strengthen the people's guardians.

It was reported that Aggulli asked the venerable elder, "Has it escaped our master's attention that sword blades that stay hidden in their scabbards for long periods rust? What then will happen to these blades if they are thrust into the shadows of walls for an even longer time?" The group liked this riposte and repeated it to their wives in the privacy of their homes. Then it journeyed from these women's tongues to the markets and from there found its way beyond the walls. The tribes praised it and other tribes adopted it as an argument in favor of their animosity to sedentary life and to settling down on the earth.

But this report also stated that Emmamma did not yield that day. Instead he stretched out his thin fingers, which resembled twigs, to pull the edge of his blue veil down over his small eyes, which were concealed by veils of blindness, and swayed back and forth before releasing a moan, which emanated from the land of eternity, asking, "Can't you discover a technique to protect blades against rust?" The assembled men released murmurs of approval and also swayed back and forth ecstatically, whether from despair, desire for glorious past travels, or a hope for release from the bondage of the lowlands.

Then Aggulli replied with a cryptic phrase that channeled the calamity of the past and the calamities of times to come: "Far from it, Master. How preposterous!"

7

The wall extended from the northern heights, ran straight east where the earth dipped to make a hollow for the waters of Retem Valley, and wound toward the southern depressions to enclose groves of *nab'* trees and date palms as well as the fields of crops. The Oases Gate was erected in this area, and through it entered caravans arriving from the forestlands and the Southern oases. The wall subsequently circled round to include the open space of the market and proceeded west to claim ancient plains where in earlier times truffles had grown in profusion. It finally reached the Western Hammada Gate, through which the salt caravans from Majazzen entered. The oasis also greeted caravans from the North there. Next the awe-inspiring wall continued its course northward to take in the masses of houses built on the heights, before terminating its severe, circular course at the place where the circular temple stood. Discriminating people discerned in this correspondence a coded sign. They said that the great wall's circle was inspired by the circular shape of the noble mausoleum and that the men who had built the new structure had been inspired, perhaps unconsciously, by the plan created by the Lover of Stones.

8

Throughout this whole period, people did not simply treat Emmamma with the veneration they customarily showed toward elders and he did not merely inspire in their souls the secret dread that the sight of any person who has achieved a great age does. They viewed him, moreover, with the admiration due someone who had long struggled with time and defeated time for a long period.

In later years, when the tribe settled on the land and grew comfortable with sleeping inside walls, they noticed changes in their bodies and their souls. Then they realized that their venerable elder had already undergone these same changes. For the first time in his heroic struggle with time, he seemed to fall apart. He grew even thinner, his skin dried to his bones, and his limbs became extremely emaciated. He began to fade and fritter away. Nothing was left of his body except his enveloping veil and flowing *thawb*.

All that remained of his speech were his sorrowful moan and the sighs of lethal longing known only to one who has spent a long time alone in the wasteland or has lived as a stranger among people, because long ago he had voyaged off, entered the eternal, unknown lands, and had continued to speak to people from there. From these mysterious realms he addressed the people on the day they assembled to debate the right name for the oasis. He also wailed when he heard that they intended to call the new oasis "New Waw." He chanted his lament lugubriously and finally raised his index finger to ask them critically, "Do you want to dangle the sword of extinction over the head of your new homeland? Don't you know that those three letters have never been used to name a place on the earth without it incurring the Spirit World's curse and without the ghoul of extinction striking it?" Some people retorted that extinction was the destiny of every existing thing and that venturing out into the wasteland was an invitation to fall prey to the belly of the wasteland. By yielding to this principle they should not hope that their Waw would become immortal, because its condition would be no more privileged than all the other Waws ever founded in the desert.

Finally Aggulli asked the venerable elder, "How can we hope to preserve anything that we, who are an evanescent people, have brought into existence? How can vanishing offspring knead something transitory with their hands and shape it into immortal dough? All existing things, Master, fade away, and everyone who is born dies."

But the venerable elder, who was in immortality's homeland, did not hear. He swayed back and forth again and sought inspiration for a name for the oasis from the Unknown. "The leader caused its birth. The leader is the father of the oasis. The leader is the master of the oasis. The leader is the name of the oasis: Tan Amghar.[12] Name the oasis Tan Amghar. What a noble name! What a beautiful name!" He recited this for a long time and swayed back and forth for a long time, singing with a long moan. The noble elders did not conceal their delight with the name, but it was a name that lingered only on their lips, because the merchants with their caravans and the nomads had long since carried the name "New Waw" to the farthest nations.

---

12. Land of the Leader, the Leader's Land.

ABOUT THE AUTHOR

Ibrahim al-Koni, who was born in 1948, is a Tuareg whose mother tongue is Tamasheq. He immigrated to Switzerland in 1993 and currently resides in Spain.

Winner of the 2005 Mohamed Zafzaf Award for the Arabic Novel and the 2008 Sheikh Zayed Award for Literature, al-Koni has also received a Libyan state prize for literature and art, prizes in Switzerland including the literary prize of the Canton of Bern, and a prize from the Franco-Arab Friendship Committee in 2002 for *L'Oasis cachée*. In 2010 he was awarded the Egyptian State Prize for the Arabic Novel, and in 2011 Georgetown University organized a special conference devoted entirely to al-Koni's works.

Al-Koni spent his childhood in the Sahara Desert. Then, after working for the Libyan newspapers *Fazzan* and *al-Thawra*, he studied comparative literature at the Maxim Gorky Literature Institute in Moscow, where he also worked as a journalist. He later lived in Warsaw for nine years and edited the Polish-language periodical *as-Sadaqa*, which published translations of short stories from Arabic, including some of his own. His novels *The Bleeding of the Stone*, *Gold Dust*, *Anubis*, *The Seven Veils of Seth*, and *The Puppet* have been published in English translation. At least seven of his titles have appeared in French, and at least ten exist in German translation. Representative works by al-Koni are available in approximately thirty-five languages, including Japanese.